PROGNOSIS**CRITICAL**

ALSO BY GARY BIRKEN

PROGNOSIS
CRITICAL

GARY BIRKEN, MD

PROLOGUE

THE TOWN OF SAN FELIPE
POLOCHIC VALLEY, GUATEMALA

Danilo Leon had always been able to move from one crime to the next with little hesitation or remorse. Standing under the muted light of a crescent moon, the olive-skinned man inhaled the oily fumes of a nearby diesel engine that droned steadily. After staring down a seemingly endless line of abandoned shacks, he shifted his gaze across the street to the home of Juan Colendres.

Flicking his half-burned cigarette to the ground, he strolled across the street and gave the cracked plywood door several firm raps. While he waited for Colendres to answer, he checked the position of his Glock 26 in its armpit holster. The door opened and Leon found himself eye to eye with a pasty-faced man with a gray snarly beard. Like many other small-holder farmers of the region, Colendres had been driven from his land and into the depths of poverty by one of the many international sugar conglomerates that had gobbled up their land like a frenzied school of piranhas.

Colendres quickly stepped to one side. Without uttering a word, Leon entered the shack, reached into the inside pocket of his sport coat, and removed an envelope. The deal with Colendres had been set for weeks, but Leon kept his eyes transfixed on him, studying him for any signs that he'd had a change of heart and was prepared to do something about it.

"You're doing the right thing for your family," Leon said, placing the envelope in the palm of the man's tremulous hand. Colendres closed his hand around it, and then without so much as a backward glance, hurried from the hovel he'd been forced to call his family's home for the past two years.

The moment the door closed, Leon took a few steps forward and stopped in front of a three-legged wooden table. A few feet behind it, a small stick-fed fire crackled in a rusted-out metal stove. In the middle of the table sat a slatted wooden crate, exactly where Colendres had been instructed to leave it. With his arms at his sides, Leon cast a cold eye into the box. The light given off by the fire was limited, but it was sufficient to prove that Colendres had lived up to his end of the bargain. With the transaction completed, Leon wasted no time carefully picking up the weighty box and leaving.

The ordinary evening sounds were dampened by the monotonous whine of the diesel engine. The wind had begun to gust, adding a faint chill to the air. Carrying the box in front of him as if he were toting a load of firewood, Leon crossed the road and made his way back across the dusty field where he'd parked his rental.

Opening the back door, he lightly placed the crate on the seat. Before moving to the front, he took a final look around. He reasoned if Colendres was desperate enough to try to double-cross him, this would be the likely time and place he'd make his move. But, after scanning the area, he was convinced he'd seen the last of Juan Colendres, and that the only thing left to do was to make the delivery and collect the second half of his sizable fee.

Leon climbed into the SUV, slid the key into the ignition, and started the engine. Before pulling away, he turned on the interior lights and glanced over his shoulder. His eyes fell on the crate and the serenely sleeping infant wrapped in a tattered pink blanket. In spite of a crimson-hued birthmark over her eye, he found her cuter than most babies he'd taken the time to look at.

After a few moments, a smug grin crept to his face. Reminding himself that there was some urgency in his mission, he turned around, tightened his seatbelt, and drove away. As he thought about the windfall of money coming his way, he decided to turn down any new projects and spend some time at his favorite resort in Anguilla.

PART ONE

Shades of Betrayal

ONE

FIVE WEEKS LATER
PARKERSBURG, WEST VIRGINIA

Standing outside the law office of Miles Cunningham, Tim and Abby Gatewood exchanged a tentative look. With an encouraging smile, he held up his crossed fingers, kissed his wife on the cheek, and opened the door.

Barely raising an eye, Cunningham pointed at the two shabby wing chairs across from him.

"How was your trip?" he asked, steepling his fingers and setting his hands on his desk.

"It was fine," Abby answered.

"Where are you folks from again?"

"Portsmouth."

"That's in Indiana, isn't it?"

"Actually, it's in Southern Ohio," Abby responded.

"Oh yeah . . . Ohio. That's right."

Tim and Abby were married one month after their high school graduation. Seeing no reason to wait, they planned on a large family. After three years passed with no success, they turned to in vitro fertilization. When that failed as well, they were soon faced with the hard truth that the only avenue open to them was adoption. But, with its prohibitive costs and their tenuous financial state, the situation looked hopeless.

A few months later, Tim and Abby believed their prayers had been answered when a friend of a friend gave them Cunningham's name. Unfortunately, and unbeknownst to them, he was a lawyer of limited talents and less in the way of principles, who spent his days unscrupulously trying to prevent his practice from capsizing.

Fiddling with his bargain-basement reading glasses, Cunningham continued to review the large stack of documents in front of him.

Finally, he looked up and said, "It looks like everything's in order, so, if you'll just sign these papers, our business will be concluded." He leaned forward and handed them each a pen. Abby took it, but instead of signing it, she looked past Cunningham to the stroller sitting in front of a floor-to-ceiling bookcase crammed with legal tomes and black binders.

Because the baby was only three months old, Abby expected somebody would have accompanied her, but that obviously wasn't the case. She hadn't been involved nearly to the degree that Tim had, regarding the details of the adoption, but she understood enough of the unusual conditions not to ask any questions.

Looking through eyes made teary by a strange mixture of joy and apprehension, she set the pen down.

"Would it be okay if I held her?"

"Right after you sign the papers," Cunningham said. But Abby sat there in silence and gave no indication she was going to sign anything before she held her baby. After a brief time, Cunningham exhaled a plentiful breath and said, "I guess there's no harm. Go ahead."

She stood up and slowly made her way across the office to the stroller. Her eyes attached at once to the sleeping baby's face.

"Hi, Jenna," she whispered. With a hesitant hand, she reached down and stroked the velvety skin of her cheeks. She pulled back the silky chenille blanket and then gently lifted Jenna into her arms. She hadn't seen any pictures of the baby. It was part of the arrangement that she and Tim had agreed to. She saw the birthmark above Jenna's eyebrow, but it didn't bother her. She was still the most beautiful baby she'd ever seen. Pressing the baby to her chest, all of Abby's misgivings melted like an ice sculpture on a hot July evening.

Tim turned to Cunningham and said, "I just want to again make sure we understand exactly what's involved."

"We've been over this ground a dozen times, Mr. Gatewood. As long as everybody keeps a cool head, everything will be fine. Just sign the final documents and you're free to leave with your baby."

"When should we call you? We still don't know anything about her—"

"Don't ever contact me again for any reason," he told them. "You're acting like you didn't know the rules going into this arrangement." He leaned back in his chair and fixed his eyes on them. "Do we understand each other?"

"Yes," Tim answered.

"Good. All the arrangements have been taken care of. As we discussed, you will be contacted in the next year or two."

"She looks a little small for a three-month-old," Abby said.

"I assure you, she's perfectly healthy," Cunningham was quick to offer. "Now, if we can get on with this."

Tim stood up and motioned Abby to join him. She set Jenna back in the stroller as if she were made of the most fragile crystal. As soon as she gently tucked the blanket around her, Abby returned to her chair. Tim handed her a pen, and with no further hesitation, she signed the papers. Tim did the same. Cunningham leaned forward, and with his stubby hands, gathered up the documents and placed them in a file folder. There was no joyful smile on his face, nor did he offer his heartfelt congratulations and wish them many blissful years with Jenna at their side.

Tim and Abby walked over to the stroller, and then without so much as a glance in Cunningham's direction, they walked out of his office. The door had barely closed when he reached for his phone and tapped in a number.

"They just left," he stated. His words were still hanging in the air when he hung up.

Tapping the eraser-end of a pencil on his desk pad, he waited a minute before getting up and strolling over to the only window in the office. Looking down on Juliana Street, he saw the Gatewoods standing on the sidewalk. It was only a few seconds later when a black SUV pulled up. The curbside door opened and a man and a woman stepped out. Without stopping to speak with Tim or Abby, the woman quickly took Jenna from the stroller and placed her in a car seat. While the man was collapsing the stroller and putting it in the cargo area, Tim and Abby got into the SUV.

At the same moment Miles Cunningham was patting himself on the back for the large fee he'd already received in cash, the SUV pulled away and quickly disappeared down the street.

TWO

It was Dr. Jacey Flanigan's first day of work. Stepping off the elevator on the second floor of Manhattan Children's Heart Hospital, her mind was focused on the best way to conceal her anxiety.

After an outstanding performance as a cardiac intensive care resident at Montana Children's Hospital, Jacey had been aggressively recruited by several major children's cardiology groups across the country. But after being offered a position at the prestigious Manhattan Children's Heart Hospital, the other opportunities paled in comparison to living in New York City and working at the only children's hospital in the country devoted exclusively to the care of babies and children suffering from severe heart disease.

Jacey walked onto the unit and went directly to the nursing station where she had arranged to meet Dr. Nathan Beyer, the Chief of Cardiology.

Thirty minutes later, she was still waiting.

"First day?" came a voice with the hint of a southern drawl from behind her.

Jacey turned toward a woman who was tall, with tapered shoulders and a becoming smile.

"Is it that obvious?" Jacey asked, extending her hand.

"Andrea Wellburn. I'm the nurse manager."

"It's nice to meet you," Jacey said, guessing they were about the same age.

Andrea dropped her dimpled chin, regarding Jacey over the top of her brow-line-framed glasses.

"You must be the new superstar from Montana we've been hearing so much about?"

A slight flush spread across Jacey's face. She cleared her throat and pushed a few strands of her ash-brown hair from her forehead.

"I don't know about the first part, but I am from Montana. And I think I was more lucky than anything else, getting this job."

Andrea wagged a knowing finger in her direction.

"I assure you, luck plays no role in any physician Dr. Beyer decides to bring into the cardiology group. He only hires the elite of the elite. Our new doctors can't have just the possibility of greatness—they have to have the promise of it."

Becoming more embarrassed with each comment Andrea made, Jacey stole another peek at her watch.

"You wouldn't happen to know if Dr. Beyer is on the unit? I was supposed to meet him here about half an hour ago."

"Dr. Beyer is a great doctor, but he has a strange relationship with punctuality. If you're waiting for him, you might want to pull up a chair—you could be here a while. The last I heard, he was in the operating room doing a complicated ultrasound."

"Do you have any idea how long he might be?"

"Based on his past performance, I'd say about an hour...but that's only a guess," Andrea answered with a quick shrug. "We have five kids scheduled for surgery this week who all need their pre-op history and physical exam. If you want to get a jump on things, have at it."

Andrea's suggestion struck a chord of caution in Jacey's mind.

"It's my first day. Maybe it would be better if I waited for Dr. Beyer to—"

Placing a reassuring hand on her shoulder, Andrea said, "Dr. Flanigan, you're sitting at the grown-ups' table now. Dr. Beyer will expect you to take some initiative. I'd suggest you stop hanging out at the nursing station and get to work."

Jacey absently rubbed the back of her willowy neck as she pondered Andrea's advice. As the nurse manager, it seemed logical she'd know the way things ran on her unit.

"Well, if you think it's okay, I guess I'll get started on those workups."

"Good. You can begin in room 5. The patient's name is Jenna Gatewood. She's a sixteen-month-old who's pre-op to have her ventricular septal defect repaired on Thursday. She hasn't been too sick, so it should be a pretty straightforward operation."

"Okay, thanks."

Jacey stood alone at the nursing station, realizing the moment she'd been so anxious about was upon her. Being only a couple of minutes away from treating her first patient as a bona fide pediatric cardiologist, she felt a sudden flutter in her stomach. Trying to shake the anxiety, she started down the hall with a clear purpose in her step.

THREE

When Jacey walked into Jenna's room, she saw Abby and Timothy Gatewood sitting on a blue linen sofa watching their daughter playing with a toy phone. The moment they saw the doctor, they stood up and met her in the middle of the room.

"I'm Dr. Flanigan," she said, shaking each of their hands. "I'd like to spend a few minutes talking to you about Jenna."

"Of course," Abby said.

Speaking through tightened lips, Tim stated, "Jenna's pediatrician told us Manhattan Children's Heart was the best hospital in the country for heart surgery, and the only place we should take her."

"We're always happy to hear that we've gotten high grades from our referring pediatricians," Jacey said. "My understanding is that Jenna has a ventricular septal defect, a VSD, which is a hole between the two main chambers of her heart." Jacey turned toward Abby and asked, "Did you have any problems during your pregnancy?"

"We adopted Jenna."

"I see. How old was she?"

"Three months."

"Do you know if she had any serious problems in the delivery room or right after she was born?"

"We were told she was perfectly healthy," Tim said.

"How much regarding Jenna's condition has been explained to you?"

Tim placed his hand on Abby's forearm and answered, "We're comfortable we understand our daughter's illness, Dr. Flanigan."

Jacey was taken back by his curt answer. She also wondered if placing his hand on her arm was his signal for her to let him do the talking. In spite of Tim's claim, Jacey wanted to be certain the parents had a firm understanding of Jenna's illness. She took the next few minutes to make sure the Gatewoods were well informed regarding VSDs and the operation to correct it. To her surprise, they were anything but. Their answers to her questions were clipped and vague. But what perplexed her more was their apparent lack of apprehension about the open-heart surgery Jenna was facing. To the contrary, they seemed strangely disengaged.

Walking over to the ultrasound machine, she asked, "Are you sure you have no other questions?"

"I think we're fine, Dr. Flanigan," Tim assured her.

Just as Jacey was about to place the probe on Jenna's chest and begin the ultrasound, the door swung open and a baldheaded wiry man dressed in finely pressed dark-red scrubs came through the door.

He said nothing at first, but his face filled with anger. Folding his arms tightly in front of his chest, his eyes became transfixed on Jacey.

"Just what do you think you're doing?" he demanded.

"Excuse me?"

"Are you hearing impaired? I asked what you're doing."

"I'm . . . I'm sorry. Is there a problem?"

"I'm Dr. Gault. I happen to be this patient's cardiac surgeon."

"My name's Jacey Flanigan. I'm a pediatric cardiologist. I just recently joined the medical staff and"

"I didn't ask who you were, and I don't care if you're Marie Curie herself, reincarnated. You don't touch a patient of mine until you've cleared it with me."

Trying to steady herself, Jacey replaced the probe on the ultrasound machine and walked toward him. She felt as if his glare would melt the flesh from her face. By itself, his rudeness was shocking, but to behave in such an unprofessional manner in front of a patient's family was appalling.

Making sure her back was toward Tim and Abby, she said in a hushed voice, "I'm sorry you're so upset, Dr. Gault, but perhaps this is a conversation we should have in private."

His cheeks puffed with air. He then blew out an agitated sigh and gestured toward the door. Watching him march out of the room, Jacey warned herself not to become unglued. On the outside, she did everything in her power to appear calm; on the inside, she felt as if her heart was about to jump into her throat.

Before joining Gault in the hall, she turned back to the Gatewoods. She was hardly surprised to see the look of astonishment frozen on their faces.

In her calmest voice, she said, "I'm sorry for the interruption. I'll be back in a few minutes."

As she approached the door, Jacey focused on the best way to handle her unexpected dilemma. She wasn't without skills dealing with workplace politics, but she'd trained in a children's hospital where the physicians were civil to each other. She could recall a time or two when she had to deal with a doctor who was having a bad moment, but compared to Dr. Gault, they were all rank amateurs.

FOUR

The moment Jacey stepped into the corridor, she spotted Dr. Gault standing in an atrium at the far end of the hall. She wasted no time starting down the corridor. As she approached him, she was pleased to see nobody else was around. She had no idea if he'd had enough time to gather himself, but the last thing she wanted was to have some other parent subjected to his ill-mannered behavior.

When she walked into the atrium and he saw her, he scowled. Having no interest in throwing Andrea to the curb, Jacey decided to take full responsibility for seeing Jenna Gatewood.

"I have other things to do, so let's make this fast," he said.

"There are five admissions today, Dr. Gault. Dr. Beyer is tied up in the operating room. I thought it might be helpful to get started working them up, beginning with preparing your patient for her operation on Thursday."

"Key words being"—he formed air quotes with his fingers—"*my patient*," he told her flatly. "So, here's the message: when I need your help, I'll ask for it. You're a cardiologist, not a heart surgeon. The care of these patients is ultimately the responsibility of the surgeons, not the cardiologists, which means your role in this hospital is to serve as a consultant and nothing more."

Dumbfounded by his archaic approach to patient care, Jacey felt her blood start to simmer. But even with her rising anger, she was committed to retaining her civility, which included not allowing Gault to think for an instant that he'd rattled her.

"With all due respect, Dr. Gault. I was only examining Jenna. I had no intention of performing some risky procedure on her."

The surface veins on his neck instantly billowed.

"Don't be impertinent with me, young lady. I was operating on children's hearts when you were still jumping off the back of school buses."

Being infantilized didn't help matters, and in spite of her best efforts to the contrary, Jacey's patience was nearing exhaustion.

Before she could respond, however, she heard a voice from behind her. She recognized it as Dr. Beyer's.

"I see you two have gotten the chance to meet," he said. "Is there a problem, Adam?"

"Only if you consider your latest rookie seeing one of my patients without asking my permission a problem."

With a shallow hairline and thinned-out furrowed skin that underscored his chronically puffy eyes, Beyer looked every day of his sixty-one years. He was the long-standing Chief of the Division of Pediatric Cardiology and the one who had vigorously recruited Jacey to join his team. He was nationally recognized amongst his peers as an innovative medical scholar and outstanding clinician who'd done as much as anybody to advance the field of pediatric cardiology.

"I apologize for the misunderstanding, Adam. I'm sure you weren't aware that this is Dr. Flanigan's first day. I got tied up in the operating room helping on the Flores case and wasn't able to accompany her on rounds. I take full responsibility for the unfortunate misunderstanding."

"Are you handling me?" Gault asked with a lopsided smirk.

"I'd prefer to say that I'm trying to resolve a problem that you've brought to my attention."

"Always the diplomat, huh, Nathan?"

"If you'd like to discuss the matter further and more privately, we could go to my office."

With a snicker, Gault said, "As much as I'd love to have that conversation, I have far more important things to do with my time. But rest assured, I'll inform the other surgeons that you'll be having a serious conversation with Dr. Flanigan regarding her behavior. And that you'll educate her as to the way we do things around here." After a brief pause, he went on to say, "You know, Nathan, the last thing we need around here is another Jonathan Bice; I assume you know what I mean and that we're both on the same page."

"I understand completely, Adam."

"I certainly hope so. Now, is there anything else?"

"Only that I'd recommend we allow Dr. Flanigan to finish her workup of Jenna Gatewood and to complete the admission notes on the other new patients. I'll personally supervise," Beyer assured him.

"That's a fine idea, Nathan. I wouldn't want to compound her poor professional behavior with an error in diagnosis."

Stunned at Gault's final insult, Jacey stood there, speechless. Having come from a children's hospital where the care of the heart patients was a collegial and cooperative effort involving the heart surgeons and the cardiologists, she couldn't believe Dr. Beyer's subservient behavior. Groveling at Gault's feet like some terrified whipping boy was hardly what she expected. She was appalled he hadn't stood up to Gault and chastised him for the way he'd browbeaten a new member of the cardiology group. But at least Jacey had the presence of mind not to escalate matters by being openly critical of the way her new boss had handled the situation.

"Jacey, I know right about now you're upset and confused. But I think once we've had the chance to talk about all of this, you'll have a better understanding of how things sometimes work around here." After stealing a peek at his watch, he added, "Unfortunately, I have a rather important meeting in a few minutes, so I suggest we have that talk right before we make rounds later."

"Of course."

"Good. I'm sure you'll feel a lot better once we've hashed things out."

Still consumed with an equal mixture of confusion and anger, Jacey watched as Dr. Beyer hurried away. Realizing she had her whole career in front of her, she couldn't imagine allowing one ill-mannered buffoon like Adam Gault to screw things up for her. She could be as thick-skinned as the next person and was still willing to make a good-faith effort to adapt to MCHH's culture. What she wasn't willing to do was compromise her principles. She wasn't sure what the future held, but for the moment, she'd do her best to remain openminded and hope her altercation with Dr. Gault was just an incident and didn't reflect the way medicine was routinely practiced at MCHH.

Anxious to return to the Gatewoods' room, Jacey started back down the hall. She viewed herself as an optimistic person, but at the same time, not naive or unrealistic. Unfortunately, no matter how hard she tried, she couldn't help but wonder if accepting the job at Manhattan Children's Heart Hospital would turn out to be the most regrettable decision of her life.

FIVE

Thirty minutes late for her nephew's fifth birthday party, Laine Saunderson, with her four-year-old son Marc in tow, hurried up the flagstone path that took them to the front door of her sister's two-story center-hall colonial. The mother of two and an assistant bank manager, Laine was a master of multitasking. She had the slim arms of a ballerina and vivid green eyes that spoke to her Northern European roots. She was about to ring the bell when the front door opened and her sister stepped outside to meet her. Joanna was two years older, but Laine had always been the more grounded and diplomatic one.

"Congratulations, you made it," Joanna said.

"Very funny," Laine responded, giving her only sibling a one-armed hug and a kiss on the cheek. "I know I'm late, but since I have no excuse, what do you say just this once we skip your standard lecture on the importance of punctuality?"

"Deal," Joanna said, as they shared a giggle. She bent down, picked up Marc, and shook him until he laughed. "Is your globe-trotting husband back from Taiwan yet?"

"Not until Tuesday night."

Joanna put Marc down and knelt to his eye level. "Do you know what your Auntie Joanna has for you outside in the back?" His eyes widened. "A giant bounce house. All of your cousins are already in there, so you better get your buns out there before there's no bounce left for you."

Instead of charging toward the backyard, Marc slipped in behind Laine and held onto her legs. "Wow. Hold that enthusiasm," Joanna said, looking up for an instant and winking at her sister. She looked back at Marc. "If you just want to watch, that's okay. In a little while we're going to have a barbecue and then birthday cake for dessert."

Just at that moment, one of his older cousins ran up, grabbed Marc's hand, and led him out to the backyard.

"I'll be in the kitchen if you need anything," Laine yelled to him.

"Marc usually runs around here like a crazed banshee. What's going on?"

"I'm not sure. He hasn't been himself the last week or so."

"How so?"

"He's been sleeping a lot and not eating very well. He probably picked up a bug and is having trouble getting rid of it."

"What did the pediatrician say?"

"I haven't taken him in yet."

"Really?"

"I thought I'd just keep an eye on things for a little while longer and take him in after the weekend if he wasn't getting back to normal."

"I don't know, Laine, he looks a little pale to me. Maybe you should go sooner."

Laine looked at her sister dubiously. "Aren't you the one who's always calling me a hysterical helicopter mom who overreacts to everything?"

"Guilty," Joanna answered, taking her sister's arm. "C'mon. I've got a fresh pot of coffee in the kitchen."

They made their way into the bright yellow country-style kitchen. Joanna grabbed two mugs from the cupboard and filled them with coffee. Having more than enough things to talk about had never been a problem for them.

FIVE

They'd been sitting there for about fifteen minutes when the back door flew open, and Kit, Joanna's babysitter, burst into the kitchen. She was breathless and had a frantic look on her face.

Her eyes darted to Laine. "Something's wrong with Marc. He was bouncing with the other kids and he—he just collapsed. I—I don't think he's breathing."

SIX

Laine and Joanna jumped to their feet and charged out of the kitchen. By the time they reached the bounce house, all of the children had scrambled out and were huddled around the entrance. Laine quickly carved a path between them and climbed inside. Her eyes found Marc instantly. He was facedown in the far corner with his arms pinned under his body.

She rushed forward, but instantly lost her balance and fell to the side. Pushing herself up on all fours, she crawled as fast as she was able to Marc's side. Lightheaded from gulping one terrified breath after another, she tugged at his arms until they were free from beneath him. By spinning his shoulders, she was able to turn him over. The moment she set eyes on his face, she gasped. His lips were a pale shade of blue and his cheeks were drained of any color. His eyes were half-open and hollow, but he was breathing.

"Call 911," she screamed to Joanna. By this time, Kit had climbed into the bounce house and was only a few feet away. "Help me get him out of here."

Laine grabbed him under his arms while Kit scooped up his legs. It was a struggle, but they made their way across the undulating floor until they reached the exit.

"The paramedics are on their way," Joanna said, as she helped them move Marc out of the bounce house and onto a chaise lounge. Laine sat down next to him and cradled his upper body in her arms. Limp, and now barely breathing, he wasn't responding to her. Pulling him closer, she slowly rocked him, praying for help to arrive before it was too late.

Joanna raced around to the front of the house to meet the paramedics. Laine had never been one to embrace religion, but in just above a whisper, she begged for divine intervention to save her son's life. It seemed like an eternity, but it was only a brief time later that she heard the siren of the approaching ambulance. Another two minutes passed, and she saw the paramedics racing toward her.

"What happened?" the taller and more senior-appearing of the two asked.

"He was in the bounce house with the other kids and—and, he just collapsed," Laine said.

"Is it possible he collided with one of them and hit his head?" the paramedic asked, fitting an oxygen mask on Marc's face.

Laine's eyes shifted to Kit.

"No. I saw what happened. Marc was hardly jumping and none of the kids were that close to him," Kit insisted. "And then all of a sudden, his whole body went limp and he fell straight down on his face."

"Does he have any chronic illnesses?"

"No," Laine answered.

"Is he taking any medications?"

"None."

He turned to his partner and said, "Let's get him loaded."

"You can ride with us to the hospital," the second paramedic told Laine.

"Do you have any idea what's wrong with him?" she asked, trying to focus on him through eyes made hazy by a curtain of tears.

"I'm not certain, but it may be his heart," the first paramedic said. "The only thing that matters now is getting him to the hospital as quickly as we can."

"Which one are you taking him to?" Joanna asked.

"Island Shore Children's."

Joanna turned to Laine and hugged her. "I'll call Eric and let him know what's happening. I'll meet you at the hospital as soon as I can."

Lost somewhere between terror and confusion, Laine didn't respond in words. All she could manage was a vacant stare.

SEVEN

After a couple of hours of impatiently reading medical journals and drinking too much coffee, Jacey made her way to the physician's charting room to continue her conversation with Dr. Beyer. She arrived first, but just as she sat down at a small conference table, he came through the door. With an uneasy expression on his face, he shoved his chapped hands deep into the pockets of his white coat and took the chair across from her.

After a few moments of shuffling in his chair, the corners of his mouth curled into a benevolent smile.

"I guess right about now you're feeling a long way from Montana."

"Well, I've had smoother first days."

"Now that you've had a couple of hours to consider things, tell me your thoughts. Before I say anything, I'm interested to know how you'd like to handle the situation."

Jacey was surprised he began the conversation with a question she would have expected he'd have posed closer to the end of their talk. Perhaps he was testing her in some strange way—trying to see how she'd manage a difficult situation.

"I've decided not to dwell on what happened. Hopefully it was just a one-time unfortunate incident. I'd prefer to try and stay focused on my clinical responsibilities and hope Dr. Gault will treat me as a colleague and with more civility in the future."

Nodding slowly, Dr. Beyer said, "That's very introspective of you. I'm afraid when it comes to the way cardiologists and heart surgeons work together, different hospitals can vary quite a bit." Fiddling with his bowtie, he continued, "Don't you agree?"

"I trained at a hospital that took care of some pretty sick kids. I'd say the medical and surgical cardiologists managed to work together without a lot of drama."

"And I assure you, that's usually the way of things here. Unfortunately, I think you just caught Adam on a bad day."

"I guess that can happen to anybody," she said, more out of courtesy and an interest in defusing the situation than anything else.

"Every hospital has its hard realities and MCHH is no different. But we're different in certain ways. We did over four thousand open-heart operations last year. That's more than twice the number of any other children's hospital in the country, possibly the world. The hard reality here is that the surgeons are indispensable to our program."

"With all due respect, you make it sound as if the cardiologists are nothing more than the junior varsity."

A knowing grin spread across his face. Before replying, he thumbed at his chin a couple of times.

"Well, I've never thought of it in quite that way, but there's some truth in what you say. We cardiologists don't generate nearly the revenue for the hospital the surgeons do. So, if that means we have to be a little thick-skinned and ignore their behavior from time to time . . . well, it's just something we have to do," he explained. "You may not understand all of this right now, but in time it will become clear to you."

Jacey opted for a vanilla response and said, "I'm sure everything will work out."

She shared Beyer's optimism that she'd be able to understand the realities of the way MCHH cared for children. As long as it didn't create an untenable work atmosphere, she was confident she could adapt. Where she parted company with Beyer was the way he seemed so willing to condone certain attitudes while explaining the best she could do in return would be to perhaps overlook them. But she realized only time would tell, and she was still willing to give the position her best shot.

"I'm certainly glad we had this talk," Beyer stated, with relief in his voice. "I only wish we could have had it before your unfortunate encounter with Adam. That's my fault and I take full responsibility for not briefing you ahead of time." Without waiting for Jacey to comment, he clapped his hands together and added, "Now that we've put this unpleasant event behind us, let's concentrate on making rounds. We have a lot of patients to see."

"I'm ready," she answered, coming to her feet and doing her best to push a smile to her face.

EIGHT

It wasn't until six p.m. that Jacey finished making rounds. Mentally spent by the events of the day, she grabbed her backpack and was about to head for the elevators when Andrea approached.

"I'm really sorry about what happened today, Dr. Flanigan. If I'd had any idea—"

"You didn't do anything wrong, and please call me Jacey."

"Believe me, if I had known that asshole Gault was the surgeon assigned to the case, I never would have suggested you—"

"Don't worry about it. Dr. Beyer got involved and straightened everything out," she told her. Jacey knew it was a tiny lie, but she gave herself a pass, hoping it would ease Andrea's guilt a little.

"If it'll make you feel any better, you're not the first doctor Gault's gone off on. He's a real jerk and everybody knows it."

"That may be the case, but his name tag reads Vice Chief of Cardiac Surgery, which makes me a bottom-feeder compared to him. My only hope is that this entire mess goes away as quickly as possible."

"Bowing and scraping will make that happen sooner."

"That's too bad, because I've never been any good at groveling."

"In that case, I'd recommend keeping your head down for a while. It may take you a little while to figure out how to play the game around here."

"Which means what, exactly?"

"I think those of us who embrace the 'go along to get along' approach to surviving around here seem to fare better than those who easily express their own opinions." Andrea took a step closer and lowered her voice. "Look, this is a good place to work. But we're not a public hospital . . . so, we have to keep the surgeons reasonably happy, and corporate even happier. Sometimes that can get a little tricky."

"You're not exactly making me feel warm and fuzzy about my decision to come to New York."

"I don't think it's a matter of geography; I think it's the reality of modern health care," Andrea explained, putting her arm around Jacey's shoulder. "But I wouldn't worry about it. Once you get the hang of things, you'll be able to concentrate on taking care of sick kids and leave the politics to others."

"Sounds like a plan," Jacey said, as they shared a quick laugh. "By the way, who's Dr. Bice? Dr. Gault compared me to him. I got the feeling he doesn't hold him in very high esteem either."

"Jonathan Bice was one of our cardiologists. About a year ago, he went on vacation out west and was killed on a hike. Supposedly, he went out by himself and fell several hundred feet. By the time they found his body . . . well, I heard it was a pretty grisly sight. It hit us all very hard. He was a great doctor, but . . ."

"But what?"

"He was a bit of a rebel. To say he had his own ideas of how the service should be run would be a large understatement."

"Now I know why I remind Gault of him."

"Don't compare yourself to Jonathan," Andrea said. "You were just at the wrong place at the wrong time. Jonathan was too smart for his own good. He wouldn't play the game and seemed to enjoy locking horns with the powers that be." Andrea stopped to check a text message on her phone. "Great. I'm being summoned to the throne room by our Chief Nursing Office," she joked. "I'll see you later." She started to walk away but turned and said, "If you have time, there's a beautiful view of the Upper West Side from the atrium. Nobody's generally in there at this time of day. After the day you've had, you might want to check it out. I always find it to be the perfect place to escape and recharge my anti-stress battery."

"Thanks for the suggestion."

Jacey followed the corridor to where it ended in the atrium, the site of her discussion with Gault and Beyer. This time, she noted that the large hexagon-shaped vestibule featured a twenty-foot bay window and an in-wall waterfall. The ceiling had been decorated with re-creations of hospitalized children's drawings and finger paintings. Strolling over to the window, she gazed out at the Hudson River. Her eye was caught by a helicopter that seemed to pass right in front of her as it banked to the south and headed down the river.

She'd been staring out of the window for a few minutes when her thoughts were interrupted by the sound of a man's voice coming from the other side of the atrium. When she turned and looked in his direction, she saw Tim Gatewood sitting at one of the computer stations with his cellphone pushed against his ear. She assumed he'd arrived in the atrium after she did and neither of them had seen each other.

"I don't care how upset you are. Jenna's our daughter, and we have the right to change our minds, and there's nothing you can do about it." Jacey watched as he moved the phone from one ear to the other. "I don't appreciate your not-so-veiled threats," he said in a voice that was starting to soar. "Perhaps you should bear in mind that I've always kept our—our *business* strictly between the two of us. I shouldn't have to remind you that could change in a blink of an eye."

Even though Jacey was sure he hadn't noticed her, she felt like an intruder. She turned and backed away from the window. Starting across the atrium and toward the corridor, she caught a glimpse of Tim Gatewood. To her surprise, it wasn't anger that she saw etched on his face—it was pure desperation.

NINE

It was eleven p.m. when Jacey stepped off the elevator and began making her way to the physician charting area. She'd worked practically non-stop since arriving at the hospital at six in the morning, stopping only briefly to eat lunch and dinner. She was tired but beyond grateful that her second day had gone so much better than her first. To her relief, nobody mentioned her falling out with Dr. Gault. She'd also managed to avoid entangling herself in any other unpleasant confrontations. The day reminded her of her time at Montana Children's, where taking care of her patients was the order of the day.

She was a few steps away from the nursing station when an eager-looking young man dressed in a short white coat approached. He had narrow hazel eyes and an unflinching gaze.

"Excuse me," he said. "Would you happen to be Dr. Flanigan?"

"I am."

He extended his hand. "Liam Crawford. I'm the third-year medical student assigned to cardiology this month. The departmental administrator sent me an email yesterday telling me to meet you."

"At this time of night?"

"The email really wasn't specific about the time, but I've been in the emergency room and the interventional cardiology suite all day, so this is the first chance I've had to contact you. I asked at the nursing station, and they told me you were still here and where I could find you."

"It's nice to meet you," Jacey said, noting he looked about ten years older than the average third-year medical student. While she was a resident and fellow, Jacey had always worked closely with the medical students. Unlike some of her colleagues who regarded students as a nuisance and an annoying obstacle to getting their work done, Jacey truly enjoyed teaching.

She watched Liam fiddle with the working end of the stethoscope that he wore slung around his neck, proudly displaying it as if it were a medal. It was a common practice amongst new junior students to crow a little in celebration of leaving the classroom behind and moving to the real world of medicine.

"Is this your first clinical rotation?" she asked him.

"I'm afraid so."

"You're afraid so? You're supposed to be excited about it."

"I am, but I'm finding it a little nerve-racking."

Jacey viewed his candor as his way of warning her that he was a wet-behind-the-ears rookie and that she shouldn't expect too much from him.

"Being a little apprehensive is normal," she assured him. "Hopefully, you'll see a lot of interesting cases while you're on the service."

"I hope so. I started med school later than almost all of my classmates. I feel as if some of the professors have expected more of me because of my age."

"What did you do after college?"

"I guided whitewater rafting adventures on the Ocoee River in the Blue Ridge Mountains of Georgia."

"River guiding as a segue to med school. That's an interesting path."

"It was kind of complicated. I could explain it to you, but we'd be up all night."

Before they could get any further, a lanky and unshaven young man wearing an oversized scrub shirt and faded blue sneakers walked up.

"Dr. Flanigan?"

"Yes."

"Ron Ellis. I'm the assistant nurse manager. Sorry to interrupt, but the ER just called. They're on their way up with a four-year-old boy in cardiac crisis. He was just transferred over from Island Shore Children's. His name's Marc Saunderson." He shook his head. "As usual, they kept him too long before sending him over to us."

"Do we have a diagnosis?"

"No. All we know is that his condition is critical and deteriorating," Ron answered. "I just spoke with Dr. Wayne. He's the senior cardiologist on call with you. He's tied up in the ER with another patient. He wants you to get started and he'll join you as soon as he can." As Ron hurried off, he gave Jacey a thumbs-up. With a grin, he said, "By the way, welcome to MCHH."

Jacey looked at Liam and said, "C'mon, there's nothing like getting thrown into the deep end of the pool on your first day."

TEN

Before Jacey could organize her thoughts, the doors of the back elevator rumbled open. Two nurses pushing a stretcher hurried off the elevator and raced past her.

"Room 23," Ron announced, grabbing the stretcher's handrail to help them guide it down the hall.

Within a matter of seconds, a large company of ICU personnel converged on Marc. With Liam on her heels, Jacey followed the group. Once they were inside the room, it didn't take her long to see that everybody knew their job. But even when the responders were experienced high-performers, it didn't diminish the fever pitch that invariably accompanied a life-or-death cardiac resuscitation.

Not having enough time to formulate a step-by-step-plan, Jacey inhaled a calming breath, reminding herself she'd been in this situation before and was well trained in handling cardiac emergencies.

Feeling every pair of eyes in the room on her, she announced, "Let's get him hooked up to the monitor." Even though he was receiving a lot of oxygen, his face was pallid and his chest-wall muscles toiled to draw in each breath. Jacey's eyes flashed to the cardiac monitor. Marc's heart rate was normal, but from his dangerously low blood pressure she knew it was failing to pump a sufficient amount of blood around his body. Convinced he was moments away from a full cardiac arrest, Jacey quickly motioned to the respiratory therapist.

"Let's get him tubed. He needs to be on a ventilator right now. We're treating this as a formal code blue."

The therapist already had her lighted scope in hand. After inserting it into his mouth, she slid the plastic breathing tube into Marc's windpipe. Once it was in place and taped, she connected Marc to the ventilator. He instantly began receiving one oxygen-rich breath about every two seconds.

"Great job," Jacey told her. "We need a stat chest x-ray. And what about labs? Are they on their way?" Jacey asked, checking the settings on the ventilator.

"All of his lab work was obtained in the emergency room," came an immediate response from one of the nurses. "The results should be in the computer by now. I'll pull them up."

"Is there any history of a prior cardiac problem?" Jacey asked, noting that Marc was sweating profusely and, in spite of high ventilator settings, the oxygen level in his blood was still dangerously low.

"None, according to the mother," the ER nurse answered. "The only thing she told us was that for the past week or so he hasn't been eating well and that he's been lethargic."

Marc's cardiac problem was a complex one. With her level of concentration approaching the red line, the next couple of hours passed so quickly that Jacey lost track of the time. The cardiac medications she'd given Marc and the ventilator had finally worked together to stabilize him. He was still in critical condition, but his vital signs were finally stable and, at least for the moment, Jacey didn't fear they were at risk of losing him.

"Let's get a cardiac ultrasound on him right away," she told Ron.

"Sharon's here and ready to go," he said, waving her forward. One of the more experienced ultrasound technicians at MCHH, Sharon rolled her machine to the bedside, checked the final calibrations, and began to scan Marc's heart.

The scan continued as Dr. Beyer walked into the room.

"I just heard about this," he said. "I see that Dr. Wayne still isn't here. I'm sorry, Jacey. We should've sent someone else to help you. What can I do to assist?"

"Actually, I think we're okay for right now."

After taking a look at the monitors, he said with a wink, "I can see that. Why don't you fill me in?" Jacey took the next few minutes to thoroughly brief him on everything that had happened since Marc had arrived in the unit. "From the look of things, this young man's doing remarkably well," he said. "Take a bow, Dr. Flanigan, you've done an outstanding job." Beyer's expression of gratitude resulted in a group applause and more compliments from everybody present.

"Thank you," Jacey said, scanning the entire room. "And thank you, Dr. Beyer."

He leaned in within a few inches of her ear, and whispered, "You're not a resident anymore. Call me Nathan. You've earned it."

ELEVEN

After what may have been the most trying day of his life, Tim Gatewood boarded the Staten Island Ferry and climbed the stairs to the top deck. Over the years, he and Abby had made several visits to New York and had always stayed at his sister's home on Staten Island. Of all the many sites and activities the city had to offer, Tim's favorite was the twenty-minute ferry ride between Lower Manhattan and St. George Terminal.

As was his custom, he found a seat on one of the long benches at the bow of the boat. While he stared at the skyline of the southern tip of the city, he could feel the light chop and roll of New York Harbor. Looking to the west, he was unable to take his eyes off the Statue of Liberty. The gleaming lights that reflected off her were mesmerizing.

Because of the hour, there were only a few passengers making the ride on the top deck. He gently massaged his temple, admitting to himself that the stress of his earlier phone call had taken a sizable toll on him. He'd given up cigarettes eleven years earlier and rarely had a craving for a smoke, but at the moment nothing would have calmed him faster than to light one up.

A trim man with a ponytail plummeting from the back of his black baseball cap strolled up and sat down on the bench a few feet from him. With nobody in sight and more than ample seating on deck, Tim was hard-pressed to understand why the man had chosen to sit so close to him.

"It's quite a view," the man said.

"Yes, it is." Having no interest in making idle chitchat, Tim made it a point not to look in the man's direction.

"I take this ferry frequently. You don't look like a regular to me."

"I don't want to appear rude, but if you don't mind, I'm not much in the mood for conversation."

"Come on, Tim. It's the middle of the night and you're sitting alone on the Staten Island Ferry. Surely you can spare me a minute or two."

Turing his head sharply, Tim inquired, "I'm sorry, have we met?"

"Not formally, but we do have a mutual acquaintance."

Tim began anxiously twisting his wedding ring.

The man continued, "I'm afraid your decision has disappointed him. He was hoping that now that you've had a little more time to think things over . . . well, you might have changed your mind."

"That's not going to happen. I thought I made that clear on the phone."

"I know you did, Tim, but, again, he's hoping you'd reconsider."

"There's no way I'm going to reconsider. In fact, my wife and I are taking our daughter home later today."

In an even tone, the man suggested, "Perhaps if we—"

"I said no way and I meant it."

"I'm sorry to hear that," the man said, with a quick slap of his thighs as he slowly shook his head. "I was hoping there'd be some way we could shore up this little problem."

"Sorry, but I don't want to discuss this again."

The man stood up. "I think I can assure you of that," he said, turning toward Tim. "It's a beautiful morning. Enjoy the rest of your ride."

40

"I'm sorry you wasted your time following me all this way here, but—"

Tim's words were still hanging in the air when they were joined by the muffled sound of three hollow thuds. The pain from the nine-millimeter rounds tearing through his intestines and blowing out the front wall of the largest artery in his abdomen was excruciating. A few seconds was all it took for Tim's shirt to become saturated with the hot blood that gushed through the entrance wounds.

Between labored breaths, Tim lowered a tremulous hand to his abdomen. He slowly raised it back up to where he could see his bloodied fingers. On the bench between his inner thighs, a collection of sluggishly clotting blood swayed back and forth with the ferry's rocking. Tim struggled to keep his eyes open, but everything around him blurred into a shapeless blend of sluggishly undulating shadows. The last thing he felt before his dying heart pumped its final pint of blood was somebody pushing his shoulders against the bench behind him.

The man reached into Tim's back pocket and removed a wallet. He leaned forward so his lips were a few inches from Tim's ear.

"If you'd only been a little brighter," he said, tapping Tim a couple of times on the forehead with the corner of the wallet. He then pushed the slumping Tim back against the bench again, so he wouldn't fall to the side.

As the man walked toward the stairs, he reached up and pinched the front of his baseball cap. Being very particular about the way he wore it, he took a few seconds to tilt the visor slightly upward to the precise angle he preferred.

Five minutes later, he was off the ferry and hailing a cab. His plan was a simple one: He'd already arranged for a hotel room, where he'd get some rest until noon. After a casual lunch, he'd board the charter helicopter that had been arranged for him and return to his home in Boston. Having a hunch there would be a lot more work for him, he didn't imagine he'd be home for very long.

TWELVE

After Jacey made sure again that Marc was stable, she and Dr. Beyer went to the physician's lounge for some coffee. Before either of them could finish their first cup, Jacey received a call from Sharon asking her and Dr. Beyer to meet her at the nursing station. When they arrived, Ron and Liam were waiting as well.

"I think you may want to take a look at this," she said, handing Beyer the ultrasound images of Marc's heart she'd just finished printing. He held them up to allow both he and Jacey to study them at the same time. After a couple of moments, he pushed his reading glasses down toward the tip of his nose.

Turning to Jacey, he said, "Well, you don't see that every day."

"That's a pretty rare finding," Jacey agreed, "but based on his symptoms, it makes perfect sense. Didn't they do an ultrasound at Island Shore?"

"The nurse who gave the report to us said they did," Sharon responded, with a quick shrug. "But it's not like they have a big cardiac service. I guess they just missed it."

"Classic anomalous coronary artery with significant mitral valve damage," Beyer stated with authority. "I'd suggest we get the surgeons over here as quickly as possible. We'll need their input."

"I'll take care of it," Ron said.

"How's Marc doing?" Beyer asked.

"Rock stable," Ron answered.

"Since you've got things well under control, I guess you don't need an old curmudgeon like me hanging around. I'll see everybody later."

Jacey turned around and saw the blank look on Liam's face. Being caught up in the frenzy of the situation, she hadn't had much time for teaching.

"So, Liam," she began slowly. "Do you know what an anomalous coronary artery is?"

He pushed his lips together so hard that it practically distorted his mouth, then answered, "I have a vague recollection, but beyond that, it really doesn't ring a bell."

"Doesn't ring a bell? That's an answer we never used in my residency."

"How come?"

"Because our chief would always respond with, 'It didn't ring a bell because you don't have a clapper.'" Jacey smiled. "I only fell into that trap once."

"I'll be sure to remember that."

"Marc's major artery to his heart is in an abnormal position and not carrying enough blood, which means his heart muscle is constantly starved for oxygen. The problem usually leads to a heart attack when the person is a young adult. But sometimes the symptoms start in childhood, which is exactly what we're seeing with Marc. As time passes, his heart failure will keep getting worse."

"So, what happens next?" Liam asked.

"After we're sure he's stable, he'll need an operation to reroute his coronary arteries back to the where they're supposed to be."

"Sounds pretty risky.

"It certainly can be. A lot of heart surgeons feel it's the most difficult operation they do."

"But he's got a chance . . . right?"

"He's got a chance," Jacey assured him, having no trouble seeing he was more shaken than most medical students would be.

She reminded herself it was his first hospital rotation, and he was still getting his sea legs under him.

As Jacey and Liam were going over the events of the code blue, Ron returned.

"Excuse me, Dr. Flanigan, but do you have a moment?"

"Sure."

"Marc's mom's in the consultation room, waiting to speak with you. Her name's Laine."

"I thought Dr. Beyer already spoke with her."

"He did, but she requested that you come and talk to her also." Jacey was baffled as to why, until Ron added, "She said you two haven't seen each other in a long time, but that she knows you from college."

"Oh my God," Jacey said in just above a whisper. "Saunderson must be her married name."

"You must be right, because she said you'd know her as Laine Rehnquist."

Jacey felt her breath catch. She and Laine had met early in their first year at Northwestern. They had remained good friends until they went their separate ways after graduation. They'd stayed in touch for a year or so, but with the overwhelming demands of their professional lives, they eventually drifted apart.

Jacey's mind filled with trepidation. She hadn't spoken to Laine in years. It didn't take a member of Mensa to realize these were hardly the circumstances anybody would choose to become reacquainted with a long-lost college friend. Dreading what she knew was about to follow, Jacey started down the hall, doing everything in her power to prepare herself for what might turn out to be the most difficult conversation she'd ever had with a parent.

THIRTEEN

The instant Jacey walked into the parent consultation room, Laine stood up. Before either of them spoke, they hugged for a long time. Jacey could feel the tears on her cheeks.

"How are you doing, Lainie?"

Between a choked breath and a nervous laugh, she answered, "Nobody's called me Lainie since college."

"Let's sit down for a few minutes, so I can explain everything that's going on with Marc." Laine responded with a hesitant nod. Once they were seated, Jacey reached out and took her hands. "Marc's stable right now, but he's still very sick."

"I—I don't care how sick he is, as long as you tell me he's going to get through this okay. The doctor in the other hospital told me his heart's failing at a very fast rate."

"With the medications we're giving him, he's doing much better now. Hopefully, things will stay that way, but for Marc to fully recover, he's going to need surgery."

With a downturned gaze, Laine said, "One of the nurses in the emergency room said he might need a heart transplant."

"That's not under consideration right now," Jacey assured her. "But, as I said, he will need an operation." She then took a few minutes to thoroughly explain the procedure to Laine.

Starring down at her hands, Laine said in a monotone, "That all sounds very dangerous."

"It's a complex procedure, but the surgeons here have had a lot of experience doing it—maybe more than any other team in the country."

"My God," she muttered. "If he does pull through, how long will he be in the hospital?"

"That's impossible to say."

"Months?"

"Maybe."

"When are they planning on doing the operation?" Laine asked.

"The heart surgeons are on their way to see Marc now. It's their call, but my best guess is that they'll want to operate within the next few days."

"That soon? He's so sick. Is that safe?"

"Marc's condition is considered urgent, but the surgeons won't operate until they're sure he's ready. The sooner we start getting more oxygen to his heart muscle, the better."

"I don't think you know this, but Marc was a twin. They were premature, and Courtney got sick a few days after they were born. They told Eric and me she'd caught an overwhelming bacterial infection. The next day she went into shock . . . and a few hours later, we lost her." Laine paused long enough to look at Jacey through searching eyes. "I don't think I could find the strength to go through anything like that again."

Feeling Laine's pain to her own core, Jacey put her arm around her friend's shoulder and gently pulled her closer. As much as she wanted to offer comfort, she couldn't find the words.

"C'mon, I'll take you to see Marc. I've given you a lot to think about. We can talk more later."

"Okay."

Jacey stayed with Laine in Marc's room, answering her questions and explaining everything that was going on with his care. She soon realized, though, that Laine was exhausted and not absorbing much of what she was explaining to her.

"Why don't we go back to the parent lounge?" Jacey suggested.

When they reached the lounge, Laine's sister was waiting for her. Jacey spent a few minutes bringing her up to speed on Marc's condition and then left the two of them alone with the promise of giving them an update in an hour. As she was leaving the waiting area, Andrea called to tell her she'd assigned herself to Marc and would be caring for him until eight a.m.

Jacey stayed in the hospital to keep an eye on Marc for the next hour. When she was convinced he was perfectly stable, she gave Laine a final update and told her she'd be back in a few hours. She was on her way back to the nursing station when her phone rang. It was the heart surgeon on call, telling her he'd seen Marc, agreed with her diagnosis, and was planning to operate later that day.

Emotionally and physically exhausted, Jacey returned to her office, grabbed her backpack and left the hospital.

FOURTEEN

At a few minutes past three in the morning, Andrea finally had her first opportunity to catch up on her charting. She was in Marc's room and on the phone with the blood bank, checking on the transfusion Jacey had ordered for him, when a young man in a short pharmacy technologist's white coat came into the room. Andrea didn't recognize him, but since she worked very few night shifts, she wasn't surprised.

"Good morning," the young man said. "How's your shift going?"

Andrea ended her call and answered, "Fine, thank you." She found herself struggling to contain a smile. Maybe it was his red hair and freckles, but she couldn't believe how young he looked.

He held up a small plastic medication bag. "I have your three a.m. antibiotic."

"Special delivery? What's the occasion? Usually the pharmacy just sends it up."

"Well, we're pretty far behind tonight. When the pharmacist noticed we might be late with Marc's antibiotic, she told me to bring it straight up."

"Wow. Who's the angel working tonight?"

"I can't remember her name, but she's very nice. She said she doesn't work any weekends, so that's why I didn't know her. I usually only work weekends."

Too much information, Andrea thought to herself, walking over to him to check the medication.

"You look busy with your charting. I'll hang the antibiotic for you," he said, holding it up so Andrea could more easily confirm the patient name, medication, and dose.

"Thanks. I'm a little behind. That will be a big help."

While Andrea finished up entering her latest note in Marc's chart, the young man prepared the antibiotic by flushing the IV line with saline and hooking the bag up to Marc's IV.

"It's running in fine. You're all set," he said, heading for the door. "Have a good shift."

"Thanks. You, too."

Andrea was a "trust but verify"-type person, which prompted her to walk over to the bedside just to be certain the antibiotic was infusing properly. After checking the bag and the tubing, she was satisfied and turned her attention to drawing Marc's next set of blood tests.

Five minutes later, the young man was exiting the hospital through the emergency room. When he was three blocks away, he spotted a dumpster. After taking a quick look around, he slipped off his MCHH pharmacy jacket, and without breaking stride, he tossed it into the dumpster. Other than what he'd been taught by the man who hired him about how to hook up a medication bag and what to expect, he knew nothing about the science of medicine. He glanced down at his watch. Pleased with how well things had gone at MCHH, he grinned.

If the information he was given was correct, young Marc Saunderson was an hour or so away from departing his present life.

FIFTEEN

Jacey smacked her pillow, rolled over, and again checked the time. When she saw it was five-fifteen and that she was still wide awake, she exhaled an annoyed breath.

Knowing her chances of falling back to sleep were nil and that she was due back in the hospital in just over two hours, she threw back the down comforter she'd been sleeping under since high school and got out of bed. Having been a pediatrics resident for six years, she'd developed the skill of getting dressed for work in no time.

The moment she exited her building, Pete, the night doorman, straightened his cap and quickly approached.

"Headed to the hospital, Dr. Flanigan?" he asked, with a generous smile.

"I sure am," she answered, stepping out into the street. Pete then backpedaled toward the corner with his hand raised high and quickly flagged down a cab. Fifteen minutes later, the taxi pulled up in front of the hospital.

As soon as Jacey walked onto the unit, she spotted Marissa Parsons, one of the assistant charge nurses, sitting at the core desk, working on her laptop. When she was a few feet away, Marissa looked up, a grave expression on her face.

"You haven't heard?"

Jacey shook her head.

"Marc had a sudden cardiac arrest about an hour ago. The code-blue team's been performing CPR on him this whole time. It doesn't look good."

"Nobody called me. Who's running the code?"

"Dr. Gault."

With her heart practically jumping out of her chest, Jacey charged down the hall to Marc's room. Even though she was no stranger to the minute-to-minute uncertainty of caring for children with serious heart problems, she was still shocked that Marc had taken a sudden turn for the worse.

Having always been somebody who could check her ego at the door, Jacey considered herself as fallible as any doctor, and honest enough to admit when she'd made a mistake. But in Marc's case, she was at a loss to explain what could have possibly gone wrong. As soon as he rolled out of the elevator, they'd made a timely diagnosis and immediately instituted the most up-to-date treatment for pediatric heart failure. Marc responded to her treatment plan beyond her expectations, and when she left the hospital, he was perfectly stable.

As she expected, Marc's room was filled with all manner of medical personnel. Andrea was standing at the foot of the bed while one of the other nurses was leaning over Marc, performing chest compressions. When Jacey set her eyes on his lifeless face, the wrenching reality of the situation shook her to the bone.

"Any cardiac activity?" Gault asked.

"None, sir," one of the nurses answered.

"How long has it been?"

"We started CPR over an hour ago," came the response from the respiratory therapist.

"Let's give it another ten minutes. If we can't get any cardiac activity, I'm going to call it," Gault announced. "Give him another amp of epinephrine."

Her stomach hardened. Jacey had participated in enough code blues to recognize an exhausted and disheartened team on the verge of giving up when she saw one.

It was at that moment when Andrea gasped and pointed at the monitor. "We have a rhythm," she yelled, with two loud claps of her hands followed by a fist pump.

"It sure looks like it," Gault said.

"The blood pressure's coming up," she added.

"His heart rate's ninety and his rhythm's normal," Gault informed everybody. "You can stop the chest compressions, and somebody give me a penlight. I want to check his pupils." Andrea removed one from her pocket, clicked it on, and handed it to him. Gault leaned over and aimed the beam of light in and out of each pupil. "Not good," he said, "but hardly surprising, with a blood oxygen level so low for almost an hour. There's a good chance he's brain dead."

"What about surgery?" one of the nurses asked.

"If he's a vegetable, there's no reason to operate on him. Let's see what the neurologists have to say before making a final decision on surgery."

Jacey couldn't believe her ears. How could a physician make such a crass comment in a room full of people who'd just fought like lions, trying to save the life of a helpless four-year-old child?

"Are you going to speak to Mom?" Andrea asked him.

"Of course. Did you think I was going to send her an email?"

"Of course not, Dr. Gault. I was just checking."

Gault took off his paper surgical cap, crumpled it in his hand, and tossed it to the ground. It fell amongst dozens of empty medication boxes and other discarded supplies.

"No changes for now," he said, walking toward the door. "I'll check on him later."

Jacey was hardly shocked when he strolled past her without saying a word. She was equally unsurprised when he left the room without thanking any of the people who'd worked their butts off to save Marc's life.

SIXTEEN

After Dr. Gault left, the room cleared out quickly. With Andrea next to her, Jacey stood at the end of Marc's bed, staring at the monitors.

"I don't understand," she said to Andrea, in a voice racked with tension. "I spoke with you a few hours ago; he was totally stable. What in God's name happened?"

"I've no idea. He was doing great, then with no warning, his heart rate became irregular and his blood pressure bottomed out. The next thing I knew, he was in full cardiac arrest."

"And you're sure there was nothing at all abnormal before he coded?"

"Nothing," she said, without hesitation. "These kids are very fragile, Jacey. Sometimes, they just crash for no reason."

Jacey cast a doubtful glance in Andrea's direction. If there was one thing she'd learned from her Chief of Cardiology at Montana Children's, it was that kids don't just crash. There's always an explanation. You just have to keep looking until you find it.

"Was there a cardiologist here when Marc arrested?" Jacey asked.

"Dr. Jeune was in the unit. He responded immediately, but Dr. Gault got here a minute or so later and told him that Marc was his patient and that he didn't need any help running a code blue." She shook her head. "I don't even know what Gault was doing here in the middle of the night."

"Maybe he came in just to check on Marc."

"When one of our cardiac surgeons has a big case scheduled for the next day, they are generally at home, fast asleep," Andrea said.

Jacey again found herself baffled. She was used to the cardiologists running all of the code blues. The only time they called for a surgeon was if a patient needed an urgent trip to the operating room. Still trying to sort out what happened, Jacey started studying the empty medication boxes on the floor to see if any of them could have made Marc's condition worse. Bending down, she picked one of them up. After looking at it briefly, she tossed it into a nearby waste basket. Moving on to the next one, she did the same thing. She continued until she'd tossed the last of them into the trash.

There was a method to Jacey's madness. Marc's sudden deterioration could have resulted from several things, but one of the more likely possibilities was a medication error. Patients receiving the wrong drug or the right drug with an incorrect dose was a common cause of physician and hospital mistakes.

"Did you see any drugs Marc shouldn't have gotten?" Andrea asked her.

"Why would you ask that?"

"Because I saw you studying every medication box, and I'm not an idiot. All of those medications were given after he arrested. The code blue was already in progress."

"I understand that all of the empty boxes were from drugs normally used at a code blue. I just want to make sure he didn't receive any meds in error that could've aggravated his condition," Jacey explained, then continued by saying, "And it might not be a bad idea to look at Marc's medication record, beginning from the time he was admitted until the code blue started."

"Do you really think that's necessary?"

"It's the only way I know of to make sure he didn't receive a drug in error."

"Okay," Andrea said.

"Good. I'm going to go speak to Marc's mother. Let's meet at the nursing station in about half an hour?"

"No problem," Andrea said, "but I think we should tell Dr. Gault about the medication review before we do it. He might be offended if we don't clear things through him first."

"That's probably a good idea. From the small amount I know about Dr. Gault, I wouldn't be surprised if he pitched a fit." She shrugged her shoulders and added, "We'll just have to wait and see. I'll catch up with you in a little while."

"I might need a little extra time," Andrea said, holding up two tubes of blood. "I have to make sure these get labeled and sent over to the Research Center."

"Are they from Marc?"

"Yeah. We draw a couple of tubes of blood from any patient who has a code blue. The center uses them for various ongoing research studies."

"No problem," Jacey said, heading down the hall toward the parent lounge. She knew a medication error was a long shot, but she was concerned that something unplanned had befallen Marc after he arrived at the hospital that almost cost him his life.

As she made her way down the hall, her mind shifted to her looming conversation with Laine. She was consumed with concern that perhaps she'd been too optimistic when she'd spoken to her earlier. While Jacey pondered her possible error, she felt her stomach begin to churn.

SEVENTEEN

Jacey looked into the parent lounge and spotted Laine standing between two club chairs, shoulders stooped, staring through vacuous eyes at the far wall. After a deep breath to compose herself, Jacey headed into the lounge. Prodding her mind for any words that might diminish Laine's pain, she walked over and hugged Laine for several seconds.

"I'm so sorry, Laine," she said.

"I don't understand. Everybody said he was going to be okay. They told me we got him here on time, and that after the operation he'd be fine. Dr. Gault was just here. He told me that the operation's canceled indefinitely and that Marc may be brain dead."

"We don't know that, and it's way too early to even speculate about—"

"He also said Marc was near death from the moment he collapsed in the bounce house, and that right from the beginning he had only a small chance of surviving, even with surgery." Slowly shaking her head, she said. "I—I just don't understand how there could be so much disagreement amongst the doctors." She rocked back and forth as she spoke. "I don't know what to do. Dr. Gault practically said it would be a miracle if Marc pulled through."

Jacey understood as well as any physician that doctors had different styles when it came to speaking to a patient's family. Their degree of optimism spanned the entire spectrum from hopeless to complete confidence. But Gault's comments to Laine were so heartless that they bordered on cruelty.

"Different doctors frequently have different opinions. They can also have . . . different ways of expressing themselves. You can't give up hope," she said, careful that her voice didn't betray her disdain for Gault's crude bedside manner.

"I'd like to see my son now," Laine said. Jacey could see she was struggling to inject some strength into her voice and put on her bravest face.

"Of course," she said to Laine, finding herself almost without breath. "Would you like me to go with you?"

"I would," Laine answered, taking both of Jacey's hands in hers.

EIGHTEEN

While Jacey was talking to Laine, Andrea called Dr. Gault, who begrudgingly agreed to meet with her as soon as he'd finished his charting. She was just about to give one of her patients a medication when she caught sight of him coming out of the physician's lounge. After a mental boot in her backside for courage, she put on her game face and walked down the hall to meet him.

"Thanks for taking the time to speak with me."

"I'm pretty tired, Andrea. Are you sure this can't wait until later?"

"I just need a couple of minutes of your time."

"Fine," he said, unbuttoning his white coat and pushing his hands into the pockets. "Please make it quick."

"I was just trying to tie up some loose ends regarding Marc's code blue. Concern was raised about the circumstances of his sudden cardiac arrest. We thought we should do a thorough review of the medications he received prior to the code to make sure there were no medication errors."

"You can't be serious."

"What drugs did he receive before the code blue?"

"Basically, only an antibiotic."

"So, what's all the concern about?" he demanded. Without giving Andrea the opportunity to answer his question, he continued, "Am I missing something here? Is there some protocol or policy, which I'm unaware of, that mandates a formal drug review if a patient suffers a cardiac arrest?"

"No, but in the interest of—"

"Of what? For God's sake, Andrea, what the hell's the problem?" he asked, throwing his hands up. "The idea is as ridiculous as it is unnecessary. Just forget it." His phone rang and he raised a halting finger. "I'll be right back."

Just at that moment, Jacey walked up.

"Did you speak to him?"

"We were kind of in the middle of things when he got a call."

"How's it going?"

"Not great."

"I assumed the request would be a formality."

"You assumed wrong."

"Do you want me to wait and talk to him with you?" Jacey asked.

"I think that's probably a good idea," Andrea said, giving Jacey the high sign that Gault was approaching.

"I see our group has increased," he said, with a pinched expression.

"Good morning," Jacey said.

"Let me take a wild guess, Dr. Flanigan—this whole medication review idea is your brainchild."

"I thought it would be helpful," Jacey stated with assurance.

"Why?" he asked flatly.

"After looking through the code-blue record, I became concerned that there may have been a drug error. I'm simply suggesting we take a careful look at the meds Marc received and send a blood sample for drug levels."

"I appreciate your attention to detail, but I think we're experienced enough not to commit careless drug errors, especially in a child suffering from florid heart failure."

"I'm not implying anybody was negligent. Any hospital can make a medication mistake. How can we be sure that's not what happened unless we check?"

"Because, Dr. Flanigan, we're not just any hospital, and it's a complete waste of time." He returned his attention to Andrea. "It's been a long night and I'd like to get the hell out of here. My decision's final. It's not necessary to send a blood sample for drug level studies. You're just going to create confusion and problems we don't need." After a telling pause, he added, "Dr. Flanigan, this is your first week with us. Why don't you dial it back a notch and try staying in your own lane for a while?"

"Thank you, Dr. Gault," Andrea said, placing a restraining hand on Jacey's arm.

"So, if there's nothing else . . ."

Jacey said, "When you have time, Dr. Gault, I'd like to speak with you about the pre-operative studies and preparation regarding Jenna Gatewood's VSD repair."

"I'm not the one to speak to about that."

"Excuse me?"

"Dr. Delacour transferred Jenna's care to Dr. Nichols. He'll be the one doing the operation."

"What did Jenna's mother say? She seemed very comfortable with you."

"That's nice to hear, but I wasn't consulted about the change, so I have no idea how Mrs. Gatewood reacted. I'd add that the decision is above your pay grade, but if you have any questions, I suggest you speak with Dr. Delacour. She's the Chief of Surgery." He looked at Andrea and Jacey in turn and asked, "Does that about do it for now, ladies? I hope so, because I'd like to go home." Jacey assumed his question was rhetorical and saw no reason to respond. Turning his gaze away, he shook his head in displeasure and walked away.

Jacey again found herself confused by the way of things at MCHH. She was completely unfamiliar with patients being reassigned to a different heart surgeon for no apparent reason. It was a risky practice, as it could easily lead to miscommunication and a breakdown in the continuity of care.

Rather than dwell on it, especially since it involved Adam Gault, Jacey refocused her attention on Marc and what she could do to make sure he didn't suffer any more life-threatening complications.

NINETEEN

Abby Gatewood had always considered Tim to be the love of her life. His sudden death had left her bewildered and dazed. Between the shock of his murder, dealing with the police, and trying to keep her thoughts straight about Jenna's surgery, the preceding day had been the worst day of her life.

It was almost five p.m. and Jenna was sleeping soundly in her crib. Abby stood next to her with her eyes transfixed on her daughter's angelic face. The nurse had just left the room after taking Jenna's vital signs. Abby was content to spend some time alone with her.

After a few minutes, she reached for her phone and called Tim's brother. He informed her that he and his wife would be at the hospital in a couple of hours to spend some time with her and go over Tim's funeral arrangements. Abby was holding onto the lowest rung of the ladder, and welcomed the opportunity of spending some time with a few close family members.

She was still thinking about how nice it would be to have some family members to lean on, when she suddenly felt lightheaded. She was sure it was because she hadn't eaten since early that morning. After dipping her head forward for a minute, she felt better, but decided she needed to get something to eat. Coming to her feet, she grabbed her coat, left the hospital, and walked the one block to a small coffee shop where she and Tim had eaten a couple of times.

She chose a small table for two in the back corner of the restaurant. The server arrived tableside promptly and placed a menu in front of her.

"I know what I want," Abby said.

"I'm ready."

"I'll have the vegetable soup and half a turkey sandwich on whole-wheat toast."

The server finished taking down the order and disappeared as quickly as she'd arrived. Deep in thought, Abby aimlessly fiddled with the salt and pepper shakers in front of her. Struggling to clear her mind of recent events, she barely noticed a tall man wearing a black topcoat approaching the table.

"Hi Abby," he said, with a welcoming smile. Snapped back to the here and now, she returned the smile. But after studying his face for a few moments, she had no idea who he was. "We've never met, but I was an acquaintance of Tim's. I saw you sitting here, and I thought I'd offer my sincere regrets over his passing."

Uncertainty as to why this distinguished-looking man had suddenly appeared in the restaurant she'd chosen, or why he knew Tim had died or that she was his wife, made her leery and fearful of the situation.

"I'm sorry," she began. "I really can't seem to—"

"May I sit down for a moment?"

"Unfortunately, I won't be here very long, and I'd prefer to be alone. I'm sure you can understand."

"Of course, I do," he said, pulling out the chair directly across from Abby and sitting down. She said nothing, but her uneasiness mounted with each passing second. She took comfort in the fact that she was in a crowded restaurant.

"You didn't mention your name," Abby said.

"Suffice it to say I work with Mr. Cunningham on the adoption side of his law practice. I'm sure you remember him from Jenna's placement with you and Tim."

A wave of panic instantly penetrated her gut. She knew the color would drain from her face as it usually did when she was sufficiently scared. She started to stand up, but he quickly reached across the table and grabbed her wrist. His grasp was powerful and sent a jolt of pain up her forearm. He continued his downward pressure on her wrist until she retook her seat.

"We were always worried that Tim could be impetuous and use poor judgment. And"—he continued with an orchestrated sigh—"I'm afraid that's exactly what happened. We're hoping you don't suffer from those same fatal character flaws, and you'll listen to reason." He spoke with a plain face and a calm voice. It was as if he were blandly offering his opinion as to the best shows on Broadway. "I know I couldn't be speaking to you at a worse time, and I truly apologize, so I'll make this as brief as I possibly can."

Abby fought to steady herself. Tim had spoken to her after his argument with Cunningham. He assured her he was firm in his decision to cancel the surgery and take Jenna home. He also claimed he was unconcerned about the lawyer's bluster and veiled threats. To the say the least, she wasn't as convinced as Tim that Cunningham was all bark and no bite. From the moment she learned of Tim's death, she didn't believe for an instant he'd been mugged. Uncertain how to proceed, she hadn't shared her suspicions with the police . . . at least, not yet.

"What do you want?" she asked him.

"We'd like you to honor our agreement. If you do that, everything will be fine. We'll just pick up where we left off. You'll take Jenna home after her surgery and we'll never see or talk to each other again." He leaned back and tapped his forehead a couple of times. "It's the smart move, Abby. That is, if you're a sensible woman."

"If you're finished, I'd like to get back to Jenna," Abby said, without a particle of doubt that there was nothing idle about his threat. "All I have left in the world is Jenna and I've always been a person who's keeps her word. Does that about do it for you?"

"It certainly does, and I'm very glad you feel the way you do," he said, adding a casual smile. "And, just to show you our good faith, we're agreeable if you'd like to take Jenna home for a couple of weeks before she has her surgery. That way, you'll have time to attend to all of Tim's funeral arrangements and legal matters. As soon as you've taken care of those . . . loose ends, you can reschedule Jenna's operation. We'll even let you pick the day . . . I mean as long as you're reasonable and don't allow things to drag on too long."

"I'll take her home," she said. "I'd like to believe you that if I cooperate, you'll leave me and Jenna alone, but I guess if you want to kill me, there's nothing I can do about it."

The man came to his feet and pushed in his chair.

"For goodness' sake, Abby, what kind of people do you think we are? If you act like Tim and become a problem for us, we're not going to kill you. We're going to kill your precious Jenna."

Unable to lift her eyes to look at him, Abby barely blinked as she stared at the ground. After a mind-numbing minute passed, she finally looked up. The man was gone. Until this moment, she'd done everything in her power to hold it together, intent on not showing him any fear. But the instant she saw he was gone, she felt herself coming apart. Consumed with terror, she began sucking air as if her throat had narrowed to the size of drinking straw. While every muscle in her body stiffened with fear, she fought to fill her lungs with one controlled breath after another. Finally, after another few minutes had passed, she felt more in control, but was still hanging onto the bottom rung of the ladder. She inhaled a few more cleansing breaths, sluggishly came to her feet, and walked out of the restaurant.

TWENTY

Jacey entered the hospital, rode the elevator up to the third floor, and went straight to the unit to meet with Liam.

"Good morning," came Andrea's voice from behind her. "I just saw Liam in the back. He's printing up the latest patient list." When Jacey didn't respond, she, asked, "Jacey, are you here?"

Jacey turned toward Andrea. "Excuse me?"

"You look like you're a thousand miles away."

"I guess I have a lot on my mind."

Before Andrea could say anything more, Liam walked up. "Good morning. The first child on the list is Kurt Joseph. He's the fourteen-month-old scheduled to have his VSD repaired by Dr. Nichols tomorrow."

"Sounds straightforward," Jacey said, stealing a glance at Andrea, who was still looking at her as if she thought Jacey was in a heavy fog, detached from the here and now. "Let's have a look at his chart and then go see him."

After they completed their review of Kurt's medical records, Jacey and Liam walked to the end of the hall, knocked on the door, and entered his room.

"Good afternoon," Jacey said to Samuel and Anne Joseph. "My name's Dr. Flanigan. I'm one of the attending cardiologists. This is Liam Crawford. He's a medical student rotating on our service this month."

"It's a pleasure to meet you, Dr. Flanigan," Samuel said in a mannerly voice and giving her a firm handshake.

"We'll be doing Kurt's admission history and physical and making sure everything's in order for surgery. Dr. Nichols will be in later to see you. Where are you folks from?"

"We live right here in Manhattan," Samuel answered.

"Will it be necessary to repeat the ultrasound?" Anne asked Jacey. "The last one we did really upset him."

"According to our records, it was just done a few days ago, so we won't need to do another. When did Kurt become ill?"

"It seems like he's gotten slowly worse over the last few months." After exchanging a measured glance with her husband, Sarah said, "He's been ill on and off for a while."

"When you say worse, what kind of symptoms was he having?"

"He'd get tired a lot."

"Anything else?" she asked. Looking up from her notepad, she noticed Samuel taking a step closer to her and partially shielding his wife's body from Jacey's line of sight.

"Nothing more than the fatigue from time to time," Samuel said.

"What did your pediatrician think about his overall health?"

"We've never really had a pediatrician for Kurt. He was never sick. If we thought he needed medical care, we just took him to the emergency room here in the city."

"Which one?"

"Several different ones," Samuel answered.

"I see. And how did you come to see Dr. Nichols in his clinic?" Jacey asked, as she brought up Kurt's medical record on the laptop.

"We have a friend who's a doctor. When we told her about Kurt's symptoms, she said he might have a problem with his heart and suggested we make an appointment with Dr. Nichols.

Kurt had a lot of tests done during the appointment. I assume you have a record of them."

"I have all of his test results right here," Jacey assured him. "The ultrasound clearly shows the hole between the two chambers of his heart. The rest of his tests are all in order as well. He's a lucky guy. With a hole that large, it's amazing he didn't have symptoms months ago."

"I guess that gives us something to be thankful for," he said.

"The surgery's scheduled for Friday afternoon," Jacey stated, sensing a degree of annoyance in Samuel's tone. "I'll stop back before they take him down to the operating room just in case you have any last-minute questions."

"We would appreciate that. That's very kind of you."

Kurt began to cry. Anne quickly walked over, picked him up, and tried to console him by placing a pacifier in his mouth and slowly rocking him. She had a pained look on her face. Samuel joined her and whispered in her ear. Without saying a word, she handed Kurt to him.

"Are there any other questions?" Jacey asked, as she and Liam approached the door.

"Dr. Nichols explained everything," Samuel said.

Walking down the hall to see their next patient, Jacey said nothing. She glanced at Liam. From the look on his face, she surmised he was pretending not to notice her uncharacteristic silence.

Once again, she found herself struggling to make sense of things. It was mindboggling. Was it really possible that the parents of a child who had a severe congenital heart defect and was scheduled for surgery had brought him to Dr. Nichols with no prior medical records?

TWENTY-ONE

After finishing up with Kurt, Jacey was on her way to the Radiology Department when a tall woman with a slender silhouette walked up to her. The woman wore her muted black hair pulled straight back, was impeccably dressed, and was smiling cordially.

"Jacey, I'm Alexa Delacour. I'm one of the surgeons. We haven't had a chance to meet yet."

"It's nice to meet you," Jacey said.

Dr. Delacour's reputation of being clinically brilliant and having the hands and touch of a master surgeon preceded her. Jacey was surprised Delacour hadn't mentioned her long list of titles when introducing herself. Jacey hardly objected. It was nice to see MCHH had at least one heart surgeon with some humility.

"I've had my eye on you. You've done a great job getting our patients ready for surgery."

"Thank you."

"It's certainly nice to have another woman in the cardiology department. I've been here for nineteen years, and I'll be the first to admit this is a great hospital, but our senior administrative leadership and some of my partners aren't exactly in the twenty-first century when it comes to gender equality in the workplace." They shared in a quick laugh. "Rumor has it you're a pretty avid jogger."

"Ever since junior high."

"Ever run in any marathons?"

"Several. Mostly in college. I even trained for a few triathlons."

"Listen, Sunday mornings I jog with a group of hospital folks. We know a lot of great routes in and around the city. Anytime you'd like to join us, just let me know."

"Thanks, I'll definitely take you up on that offer."

Alexa looked down at her watch and then tapped the crystal. "I hate to cut this short, but I have office hours in a little while. I better get to the operating room. I just wanted to introduce myself and say hi. Don't forget to call me about Sunday mornings."

"I won't. It was nice meeting you."

Alexa hadn't taken more than a few steps when she stopped and turned around. A slight frown settled on her face.

"I forgot to ask. How's everything with you and Adam Gault?"

"It was just a misunderstanding. I'm sure everything will be fine," Jacey answered. "I appreciate you asking."

"You know, Adam can be a bit difficult at times but he's a damn good heart surgeon. He's also been a very good vice chief. Sometimes he becomes a little stubborn and inflexible about his patients and gets carried away. I think if you give him a chance, you'll discover he's not as bad as he sometimes seems."

"I appreciate the advice."

"It goes without saying that if you have any further problems, please give me a call. In fact, if you have any issues at all, come talk with me. My door's always open."

"Thank, you," Jacey said, watching Alexa turn around and hurry down the hall.

Since the patients she'd cared for hadn't required anything more than basic medical preparation for her surgery, Jacey suspected Alexa was pouring on the praise a little heavily. Jacey assumed her motives were genuine and that she was trying to make her feel like a valued member of the team.

TWENTY-TWO

Jacey finished making rounds and told Liam she'd meet him after lunch to see the new admissions. She then went straight to the operating rooms to observe Kurt's surgery. Wearing a pair of MCHH's cardinal-red scrub suits, she tied her mask in place and quietly pushed open the door to the operating room. She was immediately greeted by the cold temperature and the sound of classical music playing in the background. Pushing herself up on her tiptoes and craning her neck, she did her best to see past the surgical team huddled around the operating table.

Kurt's procedure was already underway, as evidenced by the bypass machine's roller pumps propelling bright-red blood through a maze of clear plastic tubes and then directly into his circulation. After one cycle around his body, the blood was returned to the pump, where it was replenished with oxygen. This exact cycle would be repeated hundreds of times, until the surgeons completed the operation and took him off bypass.

Still having trouble seeing the operation, Jacey took a few steps forward, hoping to improve her view. When she did, the circulating nurse, whose name tag read Meredith, walked over to her.

"Excuse me, but is there something I can help you with?"

"I'm Dr. Flanigan. I'm one of the cardiologists taking care of Kurt. I'm here to observe the surgery."

"I'm sorry, but I'll have to ask you to leave."

"I beg your pardon?"

"Dr. Nichols doesn't allow observers. You'll have to leave."

"I don't think you understand. I'm not an observer—I'm one of the cardiologists taking care of this patient."

"Actually, you're the one who doesn't understand. Dr. Nichols doesn't allow anybody besides his surgical team in the operating room."

Trying not to let her frustration eclipse professional behavior, Jacey said, "Supposing the patient needs an ultrasound during the operation and one of the cardiologists is needed?"

"If Dr. Nichols feels he needs the assistance of a cardiologist, he'll call for one," Meredith explained. "He's inflexible on this matter, and I'm far too busy to debate it with you any further. If you have a problem, I suggest you take it up with him after the operation. But for now, I'm asking you to respect his rules and leave the OR at once."

Astonished, Jacey looked over at Nichols. He was wearing magnifying operating glasses with his head bent over the operative field. She assumed he was oblivious to her presence. As annoyed as she was, Jacey had the sense not to interrupt him in the middle of a delicate heart operation to request he grant her an exception to his policy.

"For God's sake, Meredith, what's all the chatter about over there?" Nichols asked.

"Nothing, sir. We have an observer in the room, but everything's been taken care of," she answered, swinging a stern gaze squarely at Jacey.

Seeing no alternative, Jacey turned and walked out of the operating room without uttering another word.

TWENTY-THREE

Jacey's first reaction to being unceremoniously dismissed from the operating room was she should report the matter to Dr. Beyer. But after giving the notion some further thought, and recalling how he handled her squabble with Dr. Gault, she seriously doubted he'd have a sympathetic ear.

"Let me guess. You got tossed out of Nichols's OR," came a voice from behind her. She turned and looked at the young man dressed in rumpled scrubs that were at least two sizes too big for him.

"Mitch Laraby," he said, extending his bony-fingered hand. "Obviously, nobody gave you a heads-up regarding the old man's strict rule prohibiting observers in his operating room."

"I'm afraid not, but as of about two minutes ago, I became painfully aware of it."

"I can see that. You look a little frazzled."

"I've worked with a lot of cardiac surgeons. None of them felt the need to form an elite team and ban other doctors from the OR. How long has this been going on?" she asked, noticing his Van Dyke beard and thinking he was a bit young for the look.

"A couple of years. The policy was Dr. Nichols's overreaction to a relatively small increase in the number of post-operative infections. He claimed the numbers had gone up as the direct result of allowing too many people in the operating room. He suggested that all the surgeons adopt a similar "dedicated team and no observer" policy. The department opted to go along with the idea, deciding to use it as the basis of a research study on Dr. Nichols's higher-infection claim. They picked two surgeons—Dr. Nichols, obviously, and Dr. Corbett—to be the leaders of these elite teams. They even got corporate to go along with the idea. They handpicked all the ancillary people that would be on teams. Some of them were already working here but the others were transferred here from other hospitals."

"What was the result of the study?"

"It's still ongoing, so they haven't gathered the data or written the paper yet."

"Seems like a lot of work for a question they'll never find the answer to," Jacey stated.

"A lot of us think it was nothing more than a pity kiss from Dr. Delacour to Dr. Nichols because he is a revered senior surgeon and sacred cow around here. "

"I met Dr. Delacour. She seemed very nice and the type of person who's anxious to keep the peace," Jacey said. "I guess it all makes sense."

"Maybe so, but from an efficiency standpoint, it doesn't make sense. Neither Nichols nor Corbett will set foot in the operating room unless their crème de la crème team is scrubbed and ready to go."

"Sounds great, but what happens if one of the team members gets sick or decides to take a vacation?"

"The case gets postponed," Mitch responded. "Look, I know you've just started here, but I think you'll find that sometimes the way things are done around here is kind of like an enigma wrapped in a riddle." Mitch took a couple of steps closer. Before continuing, he took a careful look around and said, in just above a whisper, "Here's a free piece of advice: Be careful where you step. It's very easy to fall into one of the well-disguised rabbit holes—there are plenty of them." He reached into his pocket, pulled out a roll of Lifesavers, and popped one in his mouth. He offered Jacey one, but she politely waved off the offer. "I heard about your little run-in with Dr. Gault, so you must have some idea of what I'm talking about."

Not knowing Mitch well enough to jump on his bandwagon, she responded, "It was a minor mix-up. We've both moved on." She felt his skeptical eyes poring over her face.

"I'll tell you what— if you pretend you meant that, I'll pretend I believed you."

"If you don't mind me asking, how long have you worked here?" Jacey inquired.

"Two and a half years."

"I see."

"And you're wondering, if I feel the way I do, why I'm still here?"

"The thought crossed my mind, but I don't really think it's any of my business."

Thumbing his beard, he said, "It was nice to finally get a chance to speak with you. I assume I'll see you this afternoon at the weekly complications conference. I'm sure a discussion of Marc Saunderson's code blue will be on the agenda. It should be interesting, to say the least."

"I'll be there."

As Jacey made her way back down the hallway and toward the locker room, she thought about Mitch's perspective on working at MCHH. Although he didn't go into any detail about his concerns, she found herself strangely relieved to learn she wasn't the only physician who questioned some of the day-to-day practices of the hospital.

As she changed out of her scrubs, she decided it might not be a bad idea after all to brief Dr. Beyer on what happened in Dr. Nichols's operating room, before somebody else did.

TWENTY-FOUR

Just as Jacey was leaving the locker room, her phone rang. Her lips curled into a smile when she saw who was calling.

"Hi, Daddy."

"Hey, Shortcake. I was just thinking about you. I thought you'd forgotten about your old man."

Her smile grew. "I can't believe you still call me Shortcake."

"And I can't believe you still call me Daddy, so I guess we're even."

Dr. Cole Flanigan had spent his entire career in Casper, Wyoming, practicing internal medicine and cardiology. Regarded by his colleagues as a venerable member of the medical community, he preferred working alone and never considered building a mega-practice by hiring a slew of junior partners. A year ago he was diagnosed with colon cancer and had undergone extensive therapy. At the moment, he was cancer free but still under treatment.

"How are you feeling?" Jacey asked him.

"I'm fine." She wasn't surprised by his response. He didn't like to complain about the side effects of his treatment, especially with Jacey. But she knew, in spite of his claims that everything was fine, there were days that he had to struggle just to get out of bed.

He continued, "So, how's the big-time New York pediatric cardiologist doing?" With his phone pushed against his ear, he set his glass in the sink and strolled into the living room.

"Not so great. I didn't exactly hit the ground running, so I'm still kind of getting my bearings."

"You sound more than a little concerned."

"The hospital's not quite what I expected. I assumed the practice of pediatric cardiology would be the same, irrespective of geography."

"Is it the clinical practice or hospital politics that have you baffled?"

"Both. They have a real knack for making the doctors feel torn between what's best for their careers and what's best for the patients."

"Are you familiar with the philosophy of hiring slowly, but firing quickly? The principle works in both directions."

"Translate, please."

"You did a thorough job investigating the position at MCHH. If the job's not for you, politely resign and move on."

"Just like that?"

"Just like that. Listen, you know what it means to be a physician. If you're in the company of people who don't, do something about it. I didn't raise you to ignore something that's just plain wrong. Your principles only mean something when it's tough to stand by them."

"So if you were in my shoes, would you be looking for a new job, or staying on and heading in a direction that might not end so well?"

"I wouldn't look good in your shoes, plus we're not talking about me. Sorry, Shortcake, but your old man's here for advice only. You're far too old for me to be making decisions for you. I'm sure in time you'll figure things out. I know who my daughter is, and so do you."

"I love you, Daddy."

"Love you too. Stay in touch."

TWENTY-FIVE

Jacey and Liam had already seen Kurt on morning rounds, but they decided to check on him again before going to the weekly four p.m. teaching conference. The moment they stepped into Kurt's room, Jacey spotted Andrea sitting in a lounge chair, holding Kurt on her lap.

"How's he doing?"

"He's fine. Everything's in perfect order and we should be discharging him home around dinnertime."

"Really? He just had surgery yesterday."

"That may be, but this guy's good to go," Andrea said, giving him a kiss on his cheek.

"That's . . . that's amazing."

"Why? His vital signs, labs, x-rays, and heart function are all perfect. He has no fever, and he ate a big breakfast and lunch. Why keep him in the hospital?"

"If I didn't know better, I'd say he didn't have any surgery at all," Liam said.

With arched eyebrows creasing her brow, Jacey gave him a dubious look and then headed over to the laptop to have a look for herself. After she finished her review, she had to admit, Andrea's assessment of Kurt's condition was spot on. For a child who was barely twenty-four hours out from being on a cardiac bypass pump and having a large hole in his heart repaired, he looked great.

"I have to agree. He's totally recovered from his surgery."

"You seem surprised," Andrea said.

"Don't get me wrong—I couldn't be happier. It's just that every kid I've taken care of after a VSD repair has needed a few days to fully recover. I believe the average number of days in the hospital after the operation is four."

"Welcome to MCHH," Andrea said, with pride in her voice. "We do about seventy-five VSD repairs every year, which is more than any other children's hospital in the country. A lot of our kids are like Kurt. They recover with no problem and go home the next day."

"Complication-free surgery. The hospital should be commended," Jacey said, turning to Liam. "Looks like there's nothing more for us to do here. Let's head over to the conference." As they turned toward the door, it opened, and Kurt's parents walked in.

"Your son's doing great," Jacey said.

"I know. We just spoke with Dr. Nichols. We're going home later."

"I heard. I'm sure he'll give you your discharge instructions. We'll look forward to seeing you and Kurt in a couple of weeks in the clinic."

Jacey raised her eyebrows in Liam's direction. But just as she was about to leave, she stopped. "It just occurred to me that we should do a cardiac ultrasound before Kurt leaves."

"Not necessary," Andrea informed her. "Dr. Nichols always does his own. He'll be in later to take care of it."

Jacey had never worked with a heart surgeon who did their own ultrasounds. They were all done by the pediatric cardiologists. Already having expressed her surprise at Kurt's astonishing recovery, however, she saw no reason to mention this smaller thing.

Just at that moment, a tall, hook-nosed man with a slight limp approached. When he raised his eyes, a warm smile emerged.

"You must be Dr. Flanigan."

"Yes, I am."

He extended his hand. "I'm Dr. Nichols. I'm so glad I ran into you. I was going to give you a call later today. I'm so sorry about that little problem in the operating room yesterday. Meredith has been with me longer than either of us would like to admit. She tends to be a little overprotective, if you know what I mean. I call her my helicopter nurse," he said, still smiling broadly. "Thank you for your excellent care of Kurt, especially helping to get him ready for surgery."

"I was happy to be involved."

"The family was lucky to have you. Well, I guess I should go see our little patient. It was certainly nice finally getting the chance to meet you."

As soon as he disappeared into Kurt's room, Liam and Jacey shared a brief chuckle over how effusive Dr. Nichols was. He certainly was old-school, Jacey thought to herself. Although she and Liam continued to chat on their way to the conference, Jacey's mind was on Kurt. She might have been able to dismiss his remarkable recovery as an unforeseen example of good fortune, but the same wasn't true for Andrea's intriguing claim that many of the children who undergo VSD repairs at MCHH experience the same flawless recovery. Granted, the hospital had an excellent reputation and was one of the busiest children's heart surgery programs in the country. But they weren't the only hospital providing excellence in pediatric open-heart surgery. Jacey couldn't help but wonder how MCHH, doing the exact same operation as dozens of other excellent children's hospitals across the country, produced surgical results that were so dramatically better.

TWENTY-SIX

Having decided to skip lunch in favor of grabbing a tall container of coffee, Andrea and Jacey shared a wooden bench in a small tree-lined park behind the hospital. The green space was intended to provide a respite for stressed-filled parents and members of the hospital staff. It was a bright, seasonably warm day with not a breath of a breeze.

"I know you're upset about the complications conference," Andrea said.

"I'm not sure I'd even call it a conference. It couldn't have been clearer the surgeons believed that everything that happened to him was an act of God, and that the care he received was appropriate."

"What did you expect?"

"How about a little honesty and academic integrity?" Jacey answered. "I mean, it would've been nice if one of the cardiologists offered an alternative opinion."

Andrea grinned and shook her head. "Or maybe the Easter Bunny could have attended the conference and offered an opinion."

Undaunted, Jacey continued, "Forget the conference for a minute. There's something else I want to talk to you about."

"Shoot."

"I know we've already discussed the medications Marc received, but there was one other thing I wanted to ask you."

"Okay."

"Did anything out of the ordinary or unusual happen that night?"

After a few moments, Andrea slowly lowered the container from her lips. An odd look appeared on her face.

"I hadn't thought about it quite like that until you just mentioned it, but something did happen that was a little strange." Andrea turned so that she could better face Jacey. "Marc's antibiotic was due at two. Usually the pharmacy just sends it up, but because they were busy, they had one of their techs bring it up to make sure Marc got it on time."

"Why is that so unusual?"

"I'd say it happens from time to time, but that's not the strange part. The pharmacy technician offered to give the antibiotic for me. They're allowed to hang medications, but I've never actually seen one offer to do it." She tossed a light shrug toward Jacey and added, "I thought it was pretty weird at the time, but I guess I just kind of forgot about it."

"Had you'd ever seen him before?"

"Nope, never. Do you think it means anything?"

"Probably not," Jacey said, checking the time on her cellphone. "That's the only thing I can think of that was a little strange."

Jacey decided not to ask any more questions regarding Marc. Their conversation changed to more innocuous topics, and they remained in the park for another twenty minutes.

"Well, I have the afternoon off," Jacey said, "so I think I'll head home and then go for a run."

"Must be nice. But since I'm just a lowly nurse, I have to go back to work."

"I'd be happy to switch schedules with you anytime," Jacey offered, as they stood up and tossed their empty containers into a nearby trash can.

"I'll get back to you on that offer," Andrea said with a giggle. "I'll see you tomorrow morning."

Jacey made her way around to the front of the hospital to flag down a cab. She got lucky and got the first one she saw. As soon as she was inside, she reached for her phone, dialed the hospital operator, and asked to be connected to the on-call pharmacist.

"Pat Burrell."

"This is Dr. Flanigan."

"How can I help you, Dr. Flanigan?"

"I was hoping you could assist me with a medication reconciliation on Marc Saunderson for November 12."

"The four-year-old who suffered the cardiac arrest?"

"That's right."

"We do a general review of all the code-blue medications. We looked at Marc's two days ago and didn't find any problems."

"I assume that would include any possible drug errors."

"Of course. We have many minor incidents that have no effect on the patient, but they don't rise to the level of a drug error on the severity scale we use."

"Do you keep a record of the incidents as well?"

"We do, but we don't routinely include them in the type of drug review Marc had."

Even though she knew she was grasping at straws, Jacey asked, "Would you be able to check the night of Marc's code blue and let me know if there were any drug incidents?"

There was a brief pause before Pat stated, "It might help if I had an idea what you're looking for, Dr. Flanigan." There was a cautious hesitancy in Pat's tone.

"It's for med student teaching purposes. We're putting a detailed timeline together that traces the patient's medical course from the time he was admitted."

"I see. Would it be okay if I called you back in the next day or so with the information?"

"Of course, and thank you very much," Jacey said, returning her phone to her purse.

Jacey let her head fall back against the top of the seat. She'd been tempted to ask Pat if she knew the mysterious pharmacy technician Andrea told her about. But if she had already aroused Pat's suspicions, she didn't want to make matters worse. Jacey hoped Pat would never give her request a second thought, but she had no way of knowing that. In fact, for all she knew, Pat could be contacting her supervisor at this very minute.

Gazing out of the window at the crawling traffic, Jacey convinced herself that what was done was done. If Pat decided to report an odd request she'd received from a rookie cardiologist to her boss, and she got called to task on the matter . . . well, she'd just have to jump off that bridge when she got to it.

TWENTY-SEVEN

It was close to six p.m. when Jacey and Liam finished seeing their last patient of the day.

"I never thought we'd get everything done," Liam said, leaning back and stretching his arms overhead. "I'm starting to wonder if this whole medical-school idea was the right way to go." By the sarcastic grin on his face, Jacey realized he was kidding.

"I hate to spoil the moment for you, but we're not finished. We still have to review all of today's x-rays."

After a defeated sigh, he raised an index finger and said, "I have an idea. Since we skipped lunch and I'm sure we're both starving, how about grabbing a quick dinner first?"

"The doctors dining room doesn't serve dinner," Jacey reminded him. "That leaves the regular cafeteria and the vending machines. Personally, I'd rather starve to death, but you go ahead. I'll meet you back here in half an hour."

"Actually, there's alternative worth considering. Do you like pasta?"

"Pasta's like a refund check from the IRS; everybody likes it."

"I never thought of it like that," he said, with a brief chuckle. "Anyway, there's an Italian restaurant right across the street that makes great tortellini and ravioli. It's a classic neighborhood

Italian restaurant. And the service is great. We'll be back here in forty-five minutes."

Jacey had never been one to insist upon a starchy relationship with her medical students, but she'd always been mindful to maintain a level of professionalism with them. For reasons she couldn't quite get her mind around, however, she didn't feel that need with Liam. Maybe she had a higher comfort level with him because they were of similar age and loved the science and practice of medicine. Liam's suggestion to break for dinner was made even more tempting because she was as famished as he was.

"Sure, why not. But let's make it fast." As they headed toward the exit, she said, "I think I have a pretty good idea for a clinical research project. I could use some help. Are you interested?"

Liam bobbed his head up and down a few times. "Sure. What's your idea?"

"I thought it might be interesting to look at the post-op courses of the patients who have undergone VSD repairs. We could review all the cases, say, from the last three years."

After tapping at his lower lip for a few seconds, he asked, "This sudden interest in VSD repairs—I don't suppose it would have anything to do with Andrea's claim about how well the MCHH VSD-repair kids do?"

"Every good idea for a paper comes from somewhere. If MCHH's results are really as incredible as she says, it's worth reporting in a medical journal," she explained. "While I'm doing the chart review, you could pull all the articles published in the last ten years on VSD surgery."

"Don't you have to get approval from the hospital's Institutional Review Board before you start any research project?"

Jacey was surprised Liam was aware that every hospital doing research had the regulation. What he wasn't aware of was her heightened sense of urgency and her unwillingness to wait the six weeks it customarily took an IRB Committee to approve a project.

"Sometimes it's more of a guideline than a requirement."

"So, you're saying we're not going to step over the line . . . we're just going to move it a little."

"I'm sure it will be okay if we submit the proposal after we complete the chart review," she told him, pointing toward the exit. "C'mon, we can talk more about this over dinner. The sooner we eat, the quicker we can get back and review the x-rays . . . and the sooner we both can get out of here."

TWENTY-EIGHT

Jacey and Liam were waiting in front of the elevators when she caught sight of Dr. Mitch Laraby hurrying toward her. She hadn't seen him since they'd spoken outside Dr. Nichols's operating room. When he waved a frantic hand in her direction, she suspected that whatever his problem was, it was about to become hers as well.

"How are you, Mitch?" she asked with a thin smile. Seeing the frazzled look on his face, she turned to Liam. "Give me a minute. I'll meet you in the lobby."

The elevator doors rumbled open and Liam stepped aboard.

With a bit of a grimace, he said, "I'm sorry to bother you with this, but I have a favor to ask you."

"Sure, what's going on?"

"The surgeons have done it to me again. I'm kind of in a bind and could really use your help. Dr. Gault's heart transplant coordinator called me a little while ago. The organ procurement team was just notified a heart just became available in Illinois. The donor's a sixteen-year-old who was kicked in the head by a horse. It's a perfect match for the kid who's number one on our priority transplant list. The coordinator wants me to fly with the team to Illinois and stand by while they do the harvest."

"We had a pretty busy heart transplant program in Montana, but the cardiologists never went with the team to harvest an organ. I don't mean to sound insensitive, but as far as the donor's concerned, it's a little late for a cardiologist."

"Believe me, you're preaching to the choir. I don't know why they want me to go, but if I had to guess, it's probably punitive."

"What do you mean?"

"Let's just say I've been put on notice more than a few times about questioning the wisdom of our surgical colleagues. The last thing I'm going to do is challenge Gault." He paused, and with a furrowed brow, added, "I have a feeling you have an inkling of what I'm talking about."

"You could take your case to Dr. Beyer."

"He was the one who put me on notice."

Feeling as if Mitch was having trouble getting to the point, Jacey asked him flatly, "How can I help you?"

"I'm on call tonight. If you can cover my patients and any new admissions until I get back, I'd be forever grateful. And, I'll pick up one of your call days later in the month."

Being the new kid on the block, Jacey didn't feel comfortable turning down the request.

"No problem. I'd be happy to."

"Great. I'll give you a call when we're on our way back."

Mitch's eyes dropped away. Fidgeting with his watchband, an uncomfortable silence followed.

"Was there something else?" she asked, noticing a slight twitch at the corner of his mouth.

"If you have time later, there are some things I'd like to talk to you about."

"Okay."

Taking a step closer, he asked, in just above a whisper, "Do you know anything about Dr. Jonathan Bice?"

"Only that he was a cardiologist on staff here and that he died in a hiking accident."

"Jonathan and I were pretty good friends and . . . we shared some of the same concerns."

"What kind of concerns?"

"Well, this is not the kind of thing we should be talking about in the hall. Maybe we can meet for breakfast tomorrow morning."

Feeling leery about committing to the conversation, Jacey said, "Both of us may be pretty tired in the morning. Let's touch base when you get back and see how we feel."

"Okay," he responded, looking down and checking his watch. "I gotta get going," he said, hitting the button several times to summon the elevator.

Jacey was left wondering if she should have been more enthusiastic about joining Mitch for breakfast. He was obviously troubled by something, but what she saw on his face wasn't concern or anxiety—it was pure fear.

TWENTY-NINE

After seeing her fifth emergency consult and attending to a host of other patient problems, Jacey walked down to the atrium and stared out across the West Side. It was almost midnight, and she was exhausted. She was happy to help Mitch by covering his call, but she hadn't expected to face one of the busiest nights she could remember in a very long time. Still, she did find time to begin her review of the patients who'd undergone VSD repairs in the last two years.

With nothing pressing for the moment, she decided the best way to get a second wind was to get some air. Even though the hospital wasn't in a high crime area, hospital security advised those working the night shift against wandering too far from the hospital. Considering how exhausted she was, she was happy to compromise and confine her walk to the corner and back.

Jacey stepped off the elevator and made her way across the lobby. Just as she was about to walk outside, a thin man wearing a black baseball cap and a golf jacket with the collar turned up entered the lobby. A sandy blond ponytail fell from the back of his cap. Stepping aside to let him pass, Jacey couldn't help but notice his persistent stare. She averted her eyes and exited the hospital through the revolving glass doors.

She walked down a short flight of smartly polished granite steps and stopped on the sidewalk. A damp breeze from the south rose up and blew across her neck. She tipped her head back slightly, filled her lungs with the refreshing night air, and started walking toward the corner.

Looking into the storefront windows and watching the traffic pass, Jacey's mind shifted to her chart review of the VSD patients. It was uncanny, but Andrea was correct in her claim that the vast majority of VSD patients at MCHH recovered rapidly after their operation. The discovery baffled Jacey and raised the question: why would children undergoing the exact same surgery at other children's hospitals across the country have many more complications and longer hospital stays than those at MCHH?

After about five minutes, Jacey reached the corner. Feeling revitalized enough to head back to the hospital, she turned around and started back. She glanced across the street and saw the man who'd walked past her in the lobby standing between a panel truck and a late-model SUV. His eyes were riveted on her with the same menacing look on his face that she noticed when she left the hospital.

Jacey was instantly unnerved and decided to pick up her pace, but her sidelong glance of him confirmed he'd started walking faster as well. Her hope that he'd stay on his side of the street was dashed when she stole another peek in his direction and saw him jogging across the street.

It sounded like he was now about ten paces behind her. She looked down the street and then swung her gaze across to the opposite side. There was nobody else in sight. Frightened by his approach, she walked faster. But even so, she could hear his footsteps getting louder. She was tempted to make a dash for the hospital steps, but she was still too far away to outrun him if mugging or attacking her was his intent.

With each step she took, her only thought was to get back inside the hospital as fast as she was able. When she was within a few yards of the hospital steps, she stole a quick look over her shoulder. The man was still right behind her, no more than twenty feet away.

Another wave of fear shot through her. She raced to the steps. Flustered, she half missed the leading edge of the lowest step. As her foot slipped, she found herself spinning to the right. With no more than a second or two before she'd find herself upended and spread eagle on the steps, Jacey grabbed enough of the handrail to curl her fingers around it and right herself. After gulping a sharp breath, she hurried up the last few steps and bolted into the hospital.

From the lobby side of the door, she slowed her breathing and looked back toward the street. The man was on the sidewalk in front of the steps, staring back at her. His expression had changed to one of an amused smirk. Before she could avert her eyes, he raised his index finger to the brim of his New York Yankees baseball cap and gave her a small salute.

Feeling safer, she marched across the lobby to the security desk. Santiago Johns, a veteran police officer from the 31st Precinct, was working his usual Wednesday night off-duty shift. He looked up and smiled at her.

"Excuse me, Officer," Jacey began, trying her best not to sound unglued. "I was just outside for a short walk. On my way back, I—I noticed a man wearing a baseball cap following me. He kept getting closer, but I made it back here. When I got inside, I looked back, and he was staring at me from the steps." Feeling herself gulping for air and tripping over her own words, she said nothing further.

"Calm down, Doctor. I'm sure it's nothing, but I'll have a look," Johns said. "Just have a seat. I'll be right back."

Jacey sat down and nervously drummed the top of the desk. She watched as Johns exited the hospital. A couple of minutes passed, and she saw him come back through the revolving doors and return to his desk.

"There's nobody there, now, Dr. Flanigan. I'll be here until the morning. If you want to leave the building again, let me know and I'll escort you."

"Thank you, Officer, but I can't imagine ever walking outside again when I'm on call."

As Jacey walked toward the elevators, she couldn't get her mind off what had just happened. It wasn't as if she'd never been stared at by a man, but there was something different about this guy, something sinister and threatening. She tried to convince herself that he was probably just some jerk, but her blood still ran cold every time she pictured the way he stared at her.

She jumped just a little when her phone rang.

"Hi, Jacey, it's Mitch. We have the heart, and we're just about to head back to the airport. How are things in the hospital?"

"Nothing I couldn't handle."

"Good. Listen . . . I was serious about meeting this morning to finish our conversation."

"Let's decide later. It's been really busy, and if it heats up again, I may just want to go home. But call me when you get back. Have a safe flight."

Jacey rode the elevator up to the fourth floor and made her way down a narrow hallway to her on-call room and grabbed a small bottle of cranberry juice from the room's refrigerator. After the first sip, she wondered if she should take Mitch up on his offer to meet him for breakfast. Her common-sense side was begging her not to, but there was another part of her that was warning her not to pass on an opportunity that might begin to shed some light on her many unanswered questions.

THIRTY

Although there were no more new patients or emergencies in need of her on-call coverage overnight, by six a.m., Jacey was bleary-eyed from sitting in front of the computer for the rest of the shift, reviewing the charts of the VSD patients. She'd become so absorbed in her work that it never crossed her mind that Mitch hadn't called.

"You look like you just pulled an all-nighter for your organic chemistry final," came a voice from behind her. She turned in her chair and saw Liam with a container of coffee in his hand. "The nurses told me you worked all night. I don't mean to come across as too much of a brown-noser, but I thought you could use this."

"Thanks. It's definitely a suck-up move, but I'll overlook it this one time," she said, taking the container of coffee from him. "There's something I've been meaning to ask you about Marc Saunderson's code."

"Sure."

"You said something about the code-blue team drawing a couple of tubes of blood for an ongoing research study."

He nodded. "The nurse who drew the blood told one of the aides to make sure the tubes were sent to the Research Center, not the regular hospital lab."

But Jacey was distracted by the sight of Andrea coming toward her with her head bowed. When she was a few steps away, Jacey noticed her face was the color of chalk.

After a few seconds of an uneasy silence, Jacey asked, "Is there something wrong?"

Andrea scanned their faces and stated in a monotone, "You obviously haven't heard. The harvest team's plane crashed on the way back from Illinois." With a voice that cracked with each word, she added, "Everybody aboard was killed."

"My God," Jacey said, raising her hand to her mouth.

"I—I still can't believe it. Mitch and I had lunch together yesterday. We've been good friends since he started here," she said, looking at Jacey and Liam through tear-soaked eyes.

Jacey walked over to Andrea and put an arm around her shoulder.

"I'm so sorry. Is there any chance there could be some error or—"

"There's no mistake, Jacey. It's already been on the news."

"I'm so sorry, Andrea. If there's anything I can do . . . ?"

"I wish there were," she said, opening the crumbled tissue in her hand and drying her eyes again. "How could something like this happen? I don't even know why they made him go." Without saying another word, Andrea quickly turned around and hurried away.

Still numb from the news, Jacey stared down the hall. She thought about Mitch and what she suspected his beliefs and fears were regarding unorthodox patient care at MCHH. Jacey cautioned herself about being an overdramatic conspiracist, but she couldn't help but wonder if there could possibly be any connection between the unexpected deaths of Doctors Jonathan Bice and Mitch Laraby.

THIRTY-ONE

It had been two days since Jacey had learned of Mitch's death. His tragic passing was still the talk of the hospital. When she found herself thinking about his death and MCHH's strange culture, she did everything in her power to push her misgivings from her mind and keep her focus on the care of her patients.

She had spent most of the afternoon in the large four-story clinic building across the street from the main hospital, seeing post-op patients. She was about to take a break for a few minutes when her phone rang.

"Dr. Flanigan. It's Pat Burrell from the Pharmacy Department."

"Thank you for calling. I was hoping to hear from you today," Jacey said.

"I rechecked Marc's code-blue medications and found no drug errors. But, as I mentioned, we also record every incident involving a medication, no matter how irrelevant it may seem. Drug incidents by definition are much less severe than major medication errors. So, to be thorough, I checked those as well."

"I assume you didn't find any incidents with respect to Marc's care?"

"I didn't. In fact, for the period you inquired about, there were only three incidents in the entire hospital. Two involved minor

errors in drug preparation; the other was a single dose of sildenafil that was unaccounted for."

"Unaccounted for?"

"Our records indicate that one dose was drawn up but never
administered to a patient."

Jacey's interest was piqued. She was quite familiar with sildenafil. It was used to treat high blood pressure in the lungs. It
was an excellent drug for many heart problems—but dangerous if
given to a child suffering from heart failure. If Marc had received
a dose in error, it could easily explain his cardiac arrest.

"How can you be certain the dose of sildenafil wasn't accidently administered to another patient?" Jacey inquired.

"We track every dose of medication given in the hospital.
In this particular case, it was accidently drawn up for a patient
that had been discharged a few hours earlier. The only reason it
showed up as a drug incident was because the medication was
never returned to the pharmacy department."

"What do you think happened to it?" Jacey asked.

"There are several possibilities, but I suspect one of the nurses
simply discarded it."

"How can you be certain another patient didn't receive it in
error?"

"Without the patient's name on it, it never would have cleared
all the checks we do before giving any IV drug to a patient. We
also did an audit to make sure no patient received a dose of sildenafil who wasn't supposed to."

"I see," Jacey said. "Thanks again for getting back to me. You've
been very helpful."

Jacey slowly replaced the phone in the pocket of her white
coat. She realized her imagination was probably spinning out of
control again, but she couldn't help but wonder if there was any
way the missing dose of sildenafil could have accidently been
administered to Marc. Knowing the answer to her question was
contained in two tubes of his blood being stored in the Research
Center's laboratory presented her with a difficult decision. All

she needed was a small sample of the blood in order to have it analyzed for the presence of sildenafil. Unfortunately, she was certain if she went through normal channels, she'd never receive authorization.

Her final alternative wasn't a good one: if she came up with a way to obtain the blood without permission, she could send it off to an outside laboratory for analysis. If she got caught in the process, it wouldn't bode well for her job security at MCHH.

THIRTY-TWO

It was eight o'clock on Saturday morning, Jacey's first full day off since coming to work at MCHH. Having chosen to take a run through Riverside Park, she'd finished the five miles in just under an hour. She was strolling back toward the entrance, past a grove of elm trees, when she caught sight of a man about fifty feet away, walking along the tree line in the same direction she was. From his appearance and the way he was staring at her, she recognized him at once. The dark baseball cap and his menacing stare were a dead giveaway. He was the same man who pursued her outside the hospital the night Mitch Laraby was killed.

A bolt of fear flashed down her spine. With her eyes locked straight ahead, she continued toward the exit. Forcing herself not to become unraveled, she focused on the situation at hand. She reminded herself that it was broad daylight, and that she was in the middle of a large park. After a minute, she stole another peek in the direction of the trees. Slowly narrowing the distance between them, the man walked along with her, limping ever so slightly with the same uneven step she remembered.

She breathed a sigh of relief when she saw two young men slow-jogging toward her. They were dressed in red warm-ups, chattering away and tossing a football back and forth. When they were about ten feet away, Jacey moved to the center of the path and stopped them.

"Excuse me, guys. This may sound kind of silly, but I think that man over there by the trees is following me and . . . well, he's kind of got me spooked." They both turned and looked toward the trees. The man had stopped behind a bench and was looking in the other direction. "I know it's a lot to ask, but do you think you could walk me to the entrance of the park and wait until I get a cab?"

"I think we can manage that," the shorter one said. "I'm Joe Mortenson. This is my brother Mike."

"Maybe it would be easier if I just went over there and had a word with the guy," Mike suggested.

"I don't think we need to do that," Joe said, placing his hand on his brother's arm. "You'll have to excuse Mike. He works full-time as a bouncer and is very chivalrous, but sometimes he gets carried away."

It took the three of them ten minutes to reach the entrance, where they waited until Jacey was able to flag down a cab.

"Thanks, guys," she told them. "I hope I haven't screwed up your plans too much."

"Glad we could help," Mike said.

Opening the door, she thanked them again and got in. As the taxi pulled away, she turned and looked out of the back window. The man was nowhere in sight. The farther she got from the park, the more she found herself wondering if all the events of the last several days were having a greater effect on her than she realized.

She even began questioning whether the man she'd just seen in the park was really the same one from the hospital. Letting her head fall back against the seat, she closed her eyes. For the first time, she wondered if she'd taken her worry and suspicion too far, and trying to change that mindset would be a very tough bell to unring.

THIRTY-THREE

"She seemed pretty scared," Mike said, as he and Joe retraced their steps back toward the athletic fields. "Hey," he said, pointing toward the trees. "There's the asshole."

"So?"

He tossed the ball to his brother and grinned. "I think I'll have that word with him now."

"Cut it out, Mike. The guy didn't do anything. Maybe she's a squirrel and imagined the whole thing."

"Take it easy. I just want to have a little chat with him. Go on ahead. I'll meet you at the field."

With a quick tilt of his head, Joe warned, "Listen, you're not working the door now. You can't beat the crap out of somebody just because you feel like it."

"Who said anything about beating the crap out of him? I just want to talk with him. Call it morbid curiosity."

"You're a grown man, do what you want. But if you do something dumb, I'm not going to bail your sorry ass out of jail."

"Thanks," he said, as he started toward the tree line. "I'll see you over at the field in a few minutes."

As Mike approached, the man turned and walked into the grove. Double-timing it, Mike followed him in. He thought he might lose the man, but he spotted him right away.

"Hold up a sec, buddy," Mike said, moving closer and stopping when he was eye to eye with the man. "You know, that woman was pretty upset."

"What woman?"

"The one you were following—the same one you scared half to death."

The man took a single step back and slowly shook his head.

"I don't know what you're talking about. You must have me confused with somebody else. Now if you'll excuse me, I have someplace to be."

"Maybe to terrorize some other woman."

"Yeah, that's it. I'll see you," he said with a grin, as he started to walk around Mike, who quickly stepped to the side and blocked his path. The man tried again to walk past him but this time, Mike reached out and grabbed him by the wrist.

"What's your hurry, buddy? I'm still talking to you."

With a stone-cold expression, the man casually looked down at Mike's hand. He shook his head twice and let out a long breath. In one flash of a motion, he snapped his open right hand toward Mike's face, drilling his stiffened fingertips deep into his eye sockets. The penetration instantly gouged the delicate tissues of Mike's eyes. As if he'd done the same thing dozens of times before, the man's opposite hand covered Mike's mouth, muffling his earsplitting screech.

Shoving him back against a tree, the man pivoted to one side, raised his booted right foot, and with a piston-like strike, stomped Mike squarely on his instep. The shattering of the small bones of Mike's foot created a sharp cracking sound that could be heard for five feet in every direction. Wedging his forearm under Mike's chin, he pinned Mike's head to the tree trunk for a few moments before easing his grip and allowing him to crumble to the dampened ground below.

The man dusted off his golf jacket and then stepped over Mike's torso. But before walking away, seemingly as an after-thought, he rotated half a turn to his right, raised his foot, and then with one powerful motion, drove his heel into Mike's chest wall. The force of the blow shattered three ribs and drove a dozen razor-sharp bone splinters into his lung. Barely conscious, Mike was left hacking up a frothy blood-tinged sputum and gasping for one desperate breath after another. The man reached down, rolled him over, and removed his wallet from his back pocket.

The whole encounter lasted thirty seconds. With a face devoid of any emotion, the man checked his watch and then took a look around.

He chuckled and said, "Sorry, buddy."

Carefully resetting his baseball cap just the way he liked it, he strolled away without ever looking back.

THIRTY-FOUR

THIRTEENTH DAY

It was ten p.m., and after a long day of seeing patients, Jacey stood in front of the hospital, waiting for her ride home. Exhausted, she was taken by a sinking feeling when she caught sight of Adam Gault approaching. Much to her surprise, he didn't walk past her as if she were invisible. Instead, he stopped a few feet away. Before he spoke, it crossed her mind that he might reveal a human side by expressing his sorrow over Mitch's death.

"I want to tell you something," he began calmly. "From what I've seen, you're probably a competent pediatric cardiologist, especially for somebody who just completed her training."

"Thank you," she said, even though his opinion struck her as an oblique compliment at best. If she wasn't doing her level best to avoid another unpleasant experience with him, she probably would have come up with a different response.

"You may take exception to this," he continued, "but I'm doing you a favor when I tell you that when it comes to understanding the way things work around here and how to get along, you're not too bright."

"You're absolutely right—I do take exception to that."

"I can't for the life of me figure out why in the world you'd bust into Dr. Nichols's OR like that."

"I was unaware of his policy. Let's just call it a misunderstanding." Having no interest in pursuing the conversation any further, Jacey said, "If you don't mind, Dr. Gault, I've had a long day and would like to go home. Maybe we could talk about all of my lack of political savvy at another time."

"That's exactly what I'm talking about. There's no reason to be sarcastic and dismissive," he told her. "You'd be well advised to remember that doctors with attitude problems don't last very long at MCHH."

For the moment, Jacey had the presence of mind to throttle back her mounting anger and say nothing. When she saw her ride pull up to the curb, she turned and walked away. She was reaching for the handle when Gault added, "Don't make the tragic mistake of overlooking the amount of influence the cardiac surgeons have on the administration when it comes to deciding which doctors are a good fit for MCHH and which ones aren't."

Jacey turned sharply. "And don't you make the tragic mistake of confusing my civility with weakness."

"Are you threatening me?"

"Take it as you may," she told him, opening the car door.

"I hope you still have some friends at that third-rate children's hospital in Montana you trained at, because you're going to need every one of them."

Seething from the comment and unable to keep her anger in check for another instant, she slammed the car door and stormed back across the sidewalk.

"You're nothing but a schoolyard bully and an ignorant asshole," she told him straight to his face. "Don't be foolish enough to think for even a nanosecond you can intimidate me. And in the future, keep your worthless advice to yourself." With a self-assured sneer, she thrust her extended middle finger to within an inch of his nose. Without waiting for his reaction, verbal or otherwise, she turned, walked back to the curb, and climbed into the sedan.

While Jacey struggled to rein in her rage, the driver pulled away. It took a couple of minutes, but when she was finally able to collect herself, she had no regrets about the way she'd handled Gault's insults and not-so-veiled threats about the possibility losing her job.

Looking out of the window at the storefronts and then across the Harlem River to the New Jersey skyline, she knew it was inevitable he'd go straight to Doctors Beyer and Delacour to complain about her. She was equally sure he'd put his own spin on things and that she'd find herself subjected to another captain's mast. In her heart, she knew she hadn't done anything wrong, but she was far from convinced it would be enough to save her job.

THIRTY-FIVE

FOURTEENTH DAY

Jacey and Andrea exited the Toussaint Wine Bar into a blustery November evening, crossed the street, and strolled uptown alongside a stone wall that formed the western border of Central Park. Jacey liked Andrea. They never seemed to be at a loss for things to talk about. They also had a lot in common, especially when it came to their likes and dislikes.

"That was a very therapeutic evening," Andrea said. "We should make it a rule to do this at least once a week. I'm not sure we solved all of our problems, but I'd call it a good start."

"Great choice of restaurant. The food was delicious."

"It's one of my favorites," Andrea said. "Just for the record and to let you know it didn't go unnoticed, you kind of dodged my question about you and Liam at dinner."

"It was on purpose."

"So I guessed."

"I think you're forgetting he's my medical student. There's no possibility of romance, so there's nothing to talk about."

"He's only your medical student for another few weeks. Seriously, you two make a cute couple."

"Can we talk about something else?" Jacey asked, tongue in cheek, doubting she'd be able to fool Andrea by claiming she had no romantic interest in him. For the past few years, her love life had been disappointing at best. She'd had more first dates than she'd care to admit. Looking back, she would have traded almost all of them for a quiet evening at home on the couch, watching a good pay-per-view movie and enjoying a glass of chardonnay.

"Are things getting any better for you at the hospital?" Andrea asked.

With their friendship growing and the two cosmopolitans still swimming around in her head, Jacey felt less inhibited than she might normally have about confiding in Andrea.

"I guess I'm still trying to get used to things."

"It might help if you opened your mind a little. We're not Montana Children's. Different hospitals do things in different ways. I know you're upset about Marc, but every hospital has cases that don't go well."

"I'm well aware of that."

"Obviously, you still think Marc accidently received some drug that caused the code blue." Waving her hand, Andrea continued, "Don't bother denying it. The word is out that you made some not-so-discreet inquiries about the drugs he received." Jacey was hardly surprised that her conversation with Pat Burrell hadn't remained confidential.

"I think it's a possibility that should have been ruled out. Obviously, I'm the only one."

"You have the option of bringing it up at the next complications conference."

"You mean in front of the entire medical staff," she said, with no attempt to disguise her impression that Andrea had completely lost her sense. "Perhaps you've forgotten, but I don't have 'surgeon' on my business card. I don't think any of them gives a damn about anything a cardiologist might have to say, especially one who's been on the job less than a month."

"It was just a thought."

"It's not like Marc's code blue is the only inexplicably strange thing going on at MCHH. How about the practice of banning cardiologists from the operating room?"

"A few quirky surgeons don't exactly make for a conspiracy, Jacey." Andrea paused for a few seconds and then asked, "Are you sure this isn't about Gault?"

They approached the corner and waited for the traffic light to turn green. Two cab drivers hung out of their windows, shaking their fists and hollering at each other. Still smiling at the spectacle, they hurried across the street the moment the signal changed.

"I'll be the first to admit that Adam Gault's a jerk who has all the warmth of a glacier. How he wound up caring for children is something I'll never understand. But my personal feelings toward him have nothing to do with my concerns regarding Marc's care and some of the other strange things I've seen."

"Some people would think 'strange' is doing a VSD study without the approval of the IRB Committee—don't bother trying to deny that either. Do you have any idea how much trouble you can get into?"

"I guess I'll just have to take that chance."

"Just remember, trying to keep anything a secret at MCHH is like trying to sneak the dawn past a rooster." Andrea slowed her pace and took Jacey by her arm. "C'mon, what's this research study really about? And don't give me some bedtime story that the only reason you're doing it is to write a scientific paper. If that were the case, you would have followed normal research protocols and applied for IRB approval."

"Do you really want to hear what I've found out so far?"

"Am I going to be able to stop you?" Andrea asked, but the quickly held up a hand and continued, "Sorry. Just kidding. Go ahead."

"Actually, I got the idea from you. You were the one who told me how well the VSD patients do, and you were right. No other children's hospital in the country comes close to the results MCHH gets. That concerns me."

"What the hell does that mean, Jacey? And how do you know they do better?" Andrea opened her hands and turned her palms up. "Maybe instead of being suspicious and playing private eye, you should be recommending our hospital receive a commendation. And what does all of this have to do with Marc Saunderson? He didn't have a VSD repair."

"I have different concerns about Marc's case, and actually, I'm looking at something else."

"Another unauthorized chart review?" Andrea asked, shaking a fist at Jacey.

"In the last twelve months, twenty-two children in severe cardiac crisis who needed urgent surgery were admitted to MCHH. For one reason or another, nineteen of them were transferred to other hospitals without ever having an operation."

"That's a little hard to believe."

"Check for yourself if you don't believe me. The other three died without ever going to the operating room, because they were deemed too sick to survive an operation."

"We care for some of the sickest kids in the country. We can't save them all. That's a reality of what we do, Jacey, not some gothic horror story. What I still can't figure out is why you're so obsessed with all this."

"Because something's very wrong, and maybe I'm one of the few people at MCHH who's not drinking the Kool-Aid." Jacey hesitated for a moment but then added, "Like the mysterious deaths of Jonathan Bice and Mitch Laraby."

"My God, Jacey. Just where are you going with all of this?"

"I . . . I'm not sure. Not yet, anyway."

"I don't have to tell you that if you keep all this lunacy up, you're playing Russian roulette with your career. Maybe the only thing MCHH is guilty of is setting high standards. You better start watching your butt. You wouldn't be the first doctor to be looking the wrong way when the unemployment axe fell."

The barely noticeable drizzle that started a few minutes ago was strengthening into a more substantial shower. Andrea stepped off the curb to hail a cab. After a minute, a taxi shot across two lanes of traffic and pulled up next to them. "C'mon, we'll share it," Andrea said.

"You go ahead. I'd rather walk."

"You'll get caught in a downpour."

"I'll be fine," Jacey assured her.

"Okay, but this conversation's not over."

"Why doesn't that surprise me?" Jacey asked, giving her a hug. Even though their friendship was a burgeoning one, she didn't feel for an instant that Andrea was meddling or stepping across any red lines. In some ways, having Andrea to talk to was a relief.

They waved to one another as the cab pulled away.

Paying no mind to the rain, Jacey's thoughts returned to Marc's blood sample in the Research Center. Maybe she was overthinking the risk of getting caught. After all, the building was a research laboratory, not the Pentagon. Pulling the collar of her coat higher up on her neck, she found herself wondering if quietly slipping in and out of the lab to sneak away with a small amount of blood was really as risky as she'd originally thought.

THIRTY-SIX

It was just after midnight. Jacey sat in the atrium, gazing out over the city, while she sipped on a disposable cup of lukewarm coffee. Taking the last swallow, she tossed the cup in the trash and walked out of the atrium. Instead of taking the elevator, she walked down the back stairwell and exited the hospital through the Radiology Department. She then followed a covered walkway to the six-story MCHH Research Center.

Marc's failure to improve had been the main reason prompting Jacey to make the decision to remove a sample of Marc's blood from the Research Center without approval. Her daily conversations with Laine were becoming increasingly more difficult as she struggled to keep their dialogue optimistic regarding Marc's recovery.

As part of her orientation to MCHH, Jacey had taken a tour of the modernistic research facility. Her guide emphasized that conducting high-quality research that led to important advances in pediatric cardiology care was every bit as important to the hospital's Board of Trustees as providing excellence in patient heart care.

Wearing her MCHH white coat over surgical scrubs and displaying her identification badge, Jacey assumed she'd have no difficulty reaching the elevators without attracting the attention of the security guard. Her hunch was correct, and as she strolled through the lobby past his desk and toward the elevators, the sleepy looking guard barely raised an eye in her direction.

When she stepped off on the fourth floor, she was relieved to see the area was only faintly lit and that there was nobody in sight. An acidic odor mixed with the telltale scent of ammonia draped the air. Jacey slowly made her way down the hall toward the hematology lab. When she reached the halfway point, she thought she heard a door close at the far end of the corridor. Listening intently, she stepped closer to the wall and stared down the hallway.

The chance of being seen by somebody loomed larger in her mind with each passing moment. Even though she'd thought about the possibility before she ever set foot in the Research Center, the realization that if she were discovered, she had no plausible explanation for being there, knotted her stomach.

When she heard nothing further, she again started down the hallway. With each lab she passed, she stopped to peer through the window, checking to see if anybody was working late. A sign at the end of the hall directed her to the left. As soon as she made the turn, she found herself in front of the hematology lab. Wasting no time, she opened the door and slipped inside. The lab was considerably larger than she anticipated, making the task of finding the specimen repository room containing Marc's blood samples more challenging.

With barely enough light to see her next step, she gingerly passed between two long granite-topped laboratory benches. Both were festooned with all manner of chemical reagents and scientific instruments. A few drops of perspiration rolled down her brow, finding their way into her eyes and stinging them sharply. Having no luck and realizing she was approaching the back of the shadowy lab, Jacey fought off the urge to cut and run.

The temptation evaporated when she caught sight of a door. Although the light was even more patchy in the back of the lab, she was close enough to read the name stenciled on the door:

SPECIMEN BIOREPOSITORY. After gulping a breath of relief, she placed her hand on the door handle, offered a short prayer, and gently turned it. Her prayer was answered when she met no resistance and the door easily opened. She wasted no time stepping inside.

The recessed lighting that followed the perimeter of the ceiling provided enough light for her to see. On the right side of the room stood a liquid nitrogen storage unit, used for storing blood samples that required a frozen environment. Next to it was a traditional higher-temperature refrigeration unit. The remainder of the wall space contained a series of metal racks, which housed those tubes of blood that could be maintained at room temperature. At first, Jacey was taken back by the pure number of samples, estimating there were well over a thousand of them. But when she realized they were organized by medical record number, she knew the task of locating Marc's sample, if it was there, shouldn't be that difficult.

She went right to work. Using a tremulous index finger as a pointer, she moved down one row after another. The sense of urgency that gripped her was like a sword of Damocles dangling over her head. The constant fear that somebody would suddenly come into the lab consumed her. Forcing herself to remain focused, her finger continued up and down the rows. Finally, her eyes widened as they locked onto Marc's medical record number—his two tubes of blood hadn't been discarded.

Jacey reached into her pocket and removed an empty specimen tube and a syringe. It took her only a few seconds to draw up a sample of Marc's blood and transfer it into the empty blood tube. When she was done, she carefully replaced the two tubes of blood back in the rack precisely where she'd found them. She then left the room and headed toward the entrance of the hematology lab. For the first time, she felt as if the finish line was in sight.

When she was about halfway to the door, the silence was broken by the sound of the door opening. Jacey's breath caught and she froze. Instead of swinging into a well-thought-out action plan to evade discovery, her mind turned blank. The only thing she was sure of was that if she were discovered, it would spell disaster for her.

In the next moment, she saw a flashlight beam painting the floors and benches. Feeling a cold sweat forming on the back of her neck, she assumed it was one of the security guards. Suspecting she was only a few seconds away from every light in the room coming on, she crouched down alongside the corner of the closest lab bench.

With her heart fluttering, she prayed the intrusion was the security guard making routine rounds, and after a quick look around, they would leave. Her eyes shifted to the lab bench, searching for the closest microscope station. When she spotted it, she stayed in a crouched position and silently duck-walked over to the stool that sat directly in front of the scope. Only then did she come out of her squat and sit down.

Reaching forward, she gingerly eased the base of the microscope toward her and again checked her surroundings. The flashlight beam had disappeared, but she hadn't heard the door close. She assumed the guard was still nearby. When, in the next moment, the room was suddenly awash in light, she knew she was right. Without looking around, she moved her head forward and fitted her eyes to the microscope. Battling unsteady fingers, she slid her hand to the base of the microscope.

When she heard footsteps, she looked up. A young security guard was advancing toward her. He stopped when he was a few feet away and replaced his flashlight on his leather belt. Jacey saw a casual but inquisitive look on his face.

THIRTY-SEVEN

"Good evening," Dan Marvin said. Jacey looked up again for an instant, threw a cursory wave his way, and then pretended to turn her attention back to her microscope. She hoped he'd get the message that she was working and didn't want to be disturbed. Her hopes were dashed when he added, "Working kind of late, Doctor . . . ?"

"Flanigan. I'm almost done. I only have a few more slides to review. It's hard to be a doctor during the day and a researcher at night." Deciding to take a chance, she asked him, "I thought I knew most of the night-shift security guards around here. Are you new?"

"I'm kind of new, so I get moved around a lot," he answered, taking another step forward. "Do you always work in the dark?"

"I know it seems strange, but I can see the slides better with just the light from the microscope." Jacey watched his eyes moving over her face and then dropping to her identification badge.

"If you don't mind me asking, what exactly do you do when you're not here in the lab?"

"I'm one of the cardiologists," she answered, not sure if he was doing his job or just being social.

"You must work with Dr. Delacour."

"We have some patients and research projects in common."

Before he could respond, his two-way radio squawked. Tilting his head to one side, he fiddled with the volume control. Jacey still felt his eyes all over her, maybe studying her for the truth.

"Well, Doc, I should let you get back to work."

"I appreciate it. The sooner I get out of here, the better."

He added with a wink, "Something tells me the real reason you work in the dark is because it cuts down on the interruptions."

"Busted."

"Have a nice evening."

On the one hand, Jacey was overjoyed he hadn't pushed the issue of her being there; on the other, she was far from convinced he believed her. Perhaps she was reading too much into his manner, but there was definitely a cautious hesitancy about him.

The relief she felt wasn't enough to stem the wrench-like muscle spasm building in her neck. It was a problem she'd suffered from since she'd started medical school. Whenever she had a big exam looming or one of her professors had her under the gun, the back of her neck tightened to a point where she could barely turn her head.

Marvin stopped at the door and placed his hand on the panel of light switches. Looking back at her, he asked, "Off or on, Dr. Flanigan?"

"Off, if you don't mind."

"That's what I thought."

The moment she heard the door close, her chin fell to her chest and she gasped a lungful of air. She warned herself that obsessing over the possibility Marvin would report her would serve no useful purpose. If he did, and the security department investigated her story, it wouldn't take them long to figure out she was lying. Without question, she'd be hauled in to explain what she was doing in the Research Center in the middle of the night. Her first thought was to tell the truth and accept the consequences, but the question required further reflection. At the moment, all she cared about was getting out of the building as quickly as possible.

THIRTY-SEVEN

She turned off the microscope and headed out of the lab. With her heart still pounding out of her chest from her near miss, Jacey hurried down the hall and rode the elevator to the lobby. As she headed toward the exit, she glanced over at the lobby's security guard. Pleased to see his head was still pinned behind his computer screen, she walked straight past his desk and out of the building.

THIRTY-EIGHT

As soon as Jacey was outside, she called her car service. Ten minutes later, a white SUV pulled up and she got in. She usually had the same driver. He was a talkative young guy who seemed to be a master of city driving, as evidenced by how he'd figured out how to time the stagger of the traffic lights. But this evening, a young woman was behind the wheel.

She turned around and smiled. "150 W. Amsterdam, Doctor?"

"That's it," Jacey answered.

"Late night?"

"I'm afraid so."

"Sit back and relax. I'll have you home in a few minutes."

As the car pulled away, Jacey reached for her cellphone. Her closest friend from Montana Children's, who was also studying pediatric cardiology, picked up on the second ring.

"Hi, Syd."

"My goodness," Sydnee Carlyle said. "If it isn't Jacey Flanigan herself. I thought you'd lost my phone number." Going through the rigors and trials of a pediatric residency together had made their friendship indestructible. And though it was closing in on eleven p.m. in Montana, Jacey knew Sydnee would be up and ready to talk. "So, tell me. How's life in the Big Apple?"

"Not bad. How are you doing?"

"Eight more months of this legalized slavery and I'll be done, and I can find a real job. I was considering interviewing at MCHH. What do you think?"

"Well, it has its pluses and minuses"

"That's hardly a ringing endorsement."

"It wasn't meant to be," Jacey said. "I'll fill you in on everything later, but right now I need a favor."

"Sure, what can I do?"

"I'd like to send you a blood sample. I need a complete drug panel done on it, but I'm especially interested to see if there's any sildenafil present."

"Okay . . . but aren't there about a million toxicology labs in Manhattan quite capable of running that rather basic test?"

"Yes, but I'd rather send it to you."

"Okay. From the mysterious tone to your voice, I assume you don't want this to go through normal channels."

"I'd like it handled as discreetly as possible, but I do need a written report."

"I don't have any special influence in the toxicology lab, but seeing how it's you who's asking, I'll give it my best shot."

"Thanks. I'll speak with you soon."

Jacey could feel her pulse still coming down from her experience in the Research Center. She let her head fall back against the top of the seat and closed her eyes.

THIRTY-NINE

SEVENTEENTH DAY

One week after Annalise Meehan's first birthday, her parents found themselves in New York at the office of Dr. Simon Nichols. After performing a physical examination and a cardiac ultrasound, he made the diagnosis of a VSD and scheduled her to have it repaired. Four days later, Annalise was admitted to MCHH and underwent the operation. In the recovery room, Dr. Nichols informed the parents that the procedure had been uneventful and that he anticipated Annalise would be ready for discharge the following day.

At five p.m. on the day following her surgery, Jacey and Liam walked into Annalise's room. Andrea stood next to her highchair, watching her devour a pile of chopped apples and dry cereal, before picking her up and laying her on her bed.

"She looks great," Jacey told Andrea, after checking Annalise's vital signs and listening to her heart.

"Dr. Nichols already called in to see how she was doing. He said he'd be in later to discharge her home."

"That's great news," Liam said.

Jacey was hardly astonished to learn that another VSD patient had completely recovered from surgery in less than twenty-four hours and was ready for discharge.

"Has Dr. Nichols done her discharge ultrasound yet?" she asked Andrea.

"No. He's stuck in the operating room, and I have no idea when he'll be here. It's a shame, because the Meehans have a long drive home and they'd really like to get out of here."

Having a pretty good idea of what was coming next, Jacey turned to Andrea, waved a stern finger her way, and shook her head with purpose.

"Don't even think about it, Andrea. Have you forgotten what happened to me the last time I did an ultrasound without permission?"

"I know, but this is different. Dr. Nichols is much more reasonable than Gault."

"Oh, really? Gault screamed and berated me for no reason; Nichols, on the other hand, only threw me out of his operating room."

Seeing Annalise was getting groggy, Andrea lowered her voice. "The Meehans just went to get an early dinner. They told me if the ultrasound isn't done by the time they get back, they're leaving anyway."

"That's not a problem," Jacey explained. "We can get it when she comes back for her first post-op visit."

"You're kidding, right? If I let this kid get out the door without an ultrasound, even a nice guy like Dr. Nichols will have my butt in his briefcase. C'mon, it'll take you fifteen minutes. I'll owe you one." From the pathetic look on Andrea's face, Jacey felt herself caving in.

"Fine."

Before beginning the scan, Jacey went over to the laptop station and looked at Dr. Nichols's dictated note of the operation he'd performed to repair Annalise's VSD. When Jacey walked over to Annalise's bed, she was relieved to see she was fast asleep. If things remained that way, doing the ultrasound would be a lot easier. She took the probe from Andrea and spread a generous layer of ultrasound jelly across the working end of it. Besides having a God-given talent for doing ultrasounds, Jacey had been very well trained in doing the procedure.

Jacey had only been scanning for a couple of minutes when she caught something out of the corner of her eye that struck her as unusual. She was just about to change the projection and the angle of the probe when she heard the door open. Her worst nightmare came true when she turned and saw Dr. Nichols come through the door with a perplexed expression. She couldn't help but wonder how his wrath would compare to Gault's.

"Good evening, everybody."

"I was told you'd be in the operating room for quite some time," Andrea was quick to say. "The parents have a four-hour drive and are anxious to get on the road. I asked Dr. Flanigan to do the discharge ultrasound, and she was kind enough to agree. I hope you don't mind."

He walked forward and turned off the monitor. Without being asked to, Jacey handed him the probe.

"Thanks, Jacey. That was very considerate of you to step in for me."

"I was happy to help."

"I'll take it from here. I'm kind of old-school," he said with a wink. "You know, Jacey, in the days of the giants, cardiac surgeons were actually trained and responsible for doing their own ultrasounds. I may be an old curmudgeon, but I actually prefer it that way. It's in no way a criticism of you."

Jacey was pleased to see that Dr. Nichols's polite and respectful manner was a stark departure from Dr. Gault's.

"I guess I'll get going, in that case," she said.

"Thanks again," Dr. Nichols said, busying himself with the settings on the ultrasound machine. Jacey nodded to Andrea, signaling that she and Liam would be leaving directly.

Andrea gave her a high sign to wait, then walked over and whispered, "Don't forget about our dinner plans tonight."

"I'll be there."

Even though she'd only gotten a glimpse of the ultrasound before being interrupted, Jacey couldn't shake the gnawing feeling there was something very odd about it.

FORTY

Just as Jacey stepped out of the shower and was about to get dressed to join Andrea for dinner, her phone rang. Quickly throwing on a robe, she grabbed her phone off the vanity and checked the caller ID. It was Andrea.

"Hi. I'm running a few minutes late," she told Jacey.

"No problem. We can't cancel; it's the only night we can get together for another week."

"Great. I'll see you at the restaurant."

"Wait a sec. I was just about to call you about something. Did Dr. Nichols finish the ultrasound on Annalise?"

"Yeah, the report's already on the chart. Why?"

"I want to take a look at that and the one I started and review them."

"Don't bother. Yours was deleted." When Jacey didn't respond right away, she asked, "Is that a problem?"

"I'm a little surprised."

"Why?"

"Even if it was incomplete, it's part of the patient's official medical record and shouldn't be deleted for any reason. Who deleted it?"

"I have no idea. I assume the Radiology Department did because they had a completed ultrasound done a few minutes later. If it's really bothering you, you have the option of filing an incident report."

"I can only imagine where that would take me. So if you don't mind, I'll pass on your suggestion."

"Sound thinking. You're starting to catch on to the way of things at MCHH."

"Thanks, Andrea. I'll see you in a little while."

Jacey set her phone back down and walked into the bedroom. She turned on her laptop and signed on to MCHH's electronic medical record system. It didn't take her long to open Annalise's chart and navigate to the x-ray results section. Andrea was right; the only post-operative ultrasound in the system was the one done by Dr. Nichols. There was no reference to the one she'd started. She quickly brought up the study and took a careful look at it. It looked fine to her.

Slowly walking over to her closet, she still had an uneasy feeling. But in the back of her mind, she was reminded of one of her favorite med school professors, who lectured her more than once about her tendency to overthink things. Sliding open the door, she planned and slowly smiled. For the next few hours, her only thought would be to enjoy herself, not to obsess about any of her misgivings regarding MCHH.

FORTY-ONE

By some stroke of luck, Jacey was able to complete all of her patient responsibilities by one in the afternoon. Seeing no reason to ignore her good fortune, she called it a day, slipped out of the hospital, and headed home. Before she got out of the SUV, she'd already decided to use the unexpected time off to go for a late-afternoon run. Fifteen minutes later, she was dressed and outside her building, going through her inviolate stretching routine.

She began by running north on Central Park West until she reached the American Museum of Natural History. It was an unseasonably cold day, made even more icy by a blustery wind. She'd jogged in worse weather many times in Montana, and it never crossed her mind to forgo the run because it was too chilly. As she ran, she observed for the first time the many New Yorkers bundled for winter.

Having run in place until the traffic light turned green, she crossed the street and entered a small park with well-manicured lawns, stone pathways, and a dog park. She realized that she hadn't taken time to just sit and enjoy her surroundings since arriving in New York, so she found an empty bench and sat there for a time, watching a steady stream of dog-walkers, nannies pushing strollers, and rollerbladers pass by. After a minute or so, Jacey decided this was as good a time as any to call Syd at

Montana Children's to see if she was making any progress on the blood sample Jacey had sent her.

"You must be reading my mind," Syd said. "I was going to call you after work today. I just found out that the blood you sent me tested positive for sildenafil."

Jacey bit her lip. Even though she was hearing it straight from Syd, she almost couldn't believe it.

"Was it a toxic level?"

"Nope. It was in a normal range."

"No chance of a mistake?"

"Zero. They told me they ran the assay twice. Your patient definitely had sildenafil in his blood."

"Thanks, Syd. I'll call you in a few days."

"Wait a sec, do you still want a written report?"

"Yeah, but please send it to my private email account."

"Hold it for second, Jacey. We've been friends a long time, and I'm a little worried about you. I know New York can be a mysterious place, but what's all this cloak and dagger stuff?"

"I wish I knew."

"That's not an answer."

"I really can't talk right now, but I promise I'll give you a call soon and fill you in on everything."

"Okay, but if I don't hear from you, don't be surprised if there's a knock on your door one night and you see my smiling face."

"I promise. I'll call you."

The first thing that crossed Jacey's mind was how the hospital administration and physician leadership at MCHH would react to the information. Would their concern be trying to discover what chain of events led to Marc's receiving a dangerous drug, or the best way to conceal it? Even though she'd been correct about Marc being the victim of a medication error, Jacey was sure it would pale in comparison to their demands for an explanation as to why she'd broken protocol by sending an unauthorized blood sample to another hospital. If they viewed her explanation as unacceptable, it was a certainty she'd be facing disciplinary action that could go well beyond getting written up for breaking a hospital bylaw.

With a very large threat hanging over her head, Jacey tried to calm herself and give careful thought to her situation. She stood up and began a lazy jog toward the park's exit. She realized the choice of what to do next had urgency to it, but at the same time, she was keenly aware that a poorly thought-out decision could easily make things worse. The saving grace was that there was one thing true now that hadn't been true five minutes ago: she finally had her first piece of tangible evidence that Marc had been the victim of a dire medical error.

As Jacey picked up the pace and turned east, she decided the smart move, at least for now, was to share the information with nobody.

FORTY-TWO

Jacey continued her run in a crosstown direction. Before arriving in New York, she'd researched the most scenic running routes in Manhattan. Topping many of the lists was Roosevelt Island, a two-mile-long stretch of land in the East River. The island was considered by many of its residents to be one of New York City's less celebrated treasures, being home to numerous eclectic restaurants, historic landmarks, quaint shops, and upscale residences. Of particular interest to her was seeing the Renwick Ruin, the remains of the first smallpox hospital built in the US, which dated back to the mid-1800s.

Once she reached Second Avenue, it was a short distance to the Roosevelt Island Tramway station. The wait was brief for the next gondola, which took her over to the island. She wasted no time in starting her jog along the Promenade; this path ran along the entire perimeter of the island. Once she passed the lighthouse at the north tip, she turned and started south. Dusk was just settling in, and the number of joggers and walkers had dwindled considerably. There was one jogger about ten yards in front of her who was wearing a Michigan State Lacrosse windbreaker. Glancing over her shoulder, she saw three women, who all seemed to be talking at the same time as they ran. Trailing behind them was a man in a black hooded sweatshirt.

When Jacey reached the southern tip of the island, she decided to rest for a few minutes in Southpoint Park before taking a closer look at the remains of the smallpox hospital. She found a bench, sat down, and struggled not to think about anything related to MCHH. A chilly wind rattled the last of the stubborn leaves that clung to the tree branches, sending a few of them gently spiraling to the ground. But with the shadows growing longer, she stood up and headed back toward the jogging path with the intention of taking a quick look at the smallpox hospital on her way back to the tram station.

She was only a few yards away from the hospital when the man in the black hoodie jogged up behind her. She caught sight of him out of the corner of her eye. Assuming he wanted to pass her, she moved to her right. But instead of continuing on, he slowed and ran with her step for step. When she turned her head in his direction, he suddenly grabbed her arm. The strength of his grip was crushing. Worse, though, was the sharp pain on the side of her chest from the working end of the semiautomatic that he was pushing between her ribs. She knew instantly who he was.

"If you scream or try to signal anybody, I'll kill you right here," he informed her in a relaxed tone of voice, twisting the gun deeper into the soft tissues between her ribs. "I just want your money. Play this smart, and you'll get out of this with your life."

Along with a few of her medical-school classmates, Jacey had taken a several-session women's self-defense course. She remembered her instructor's advice that when faced with being robbed, the smart thing to do was to hand over your money and valuables. But if the mugger's motive was to harm you, she advised them to fight back with every particle of strength they could muster. Jacey considered trying to pull out her pepper spray, but with the man's gun pressed against her, she quickly thought better of the idea.

"I don't have much money on me, but you can have it all and my watch. Please, just don't hurt me." Things were happening too quickly. Jacey prayed more than anything else that the man who'd been stalking her was telling the truth and all he wanted was her money. Parting with her money and watch was one thing, but if it was rape that was on his mind, she'd die before she allowed it to happen.

"Whether you get hurt or not will be entirely up to you. C'mon," he said, pushing her on. "Over that way. Remember, if you scream or try anything stupid, I'll empty this whole clip into your chest."

After no more than a dozen steps, they were within a few feet of the hospital. The majority of what remained of the Gothic-revival structure was the foundation and some decrepit segments of the ivy-covered outer walls. Terrified, Jacey's eyes darted from side to side, but she saw nobody. Even if she had, she wasn't sure, with his gun jammed into her side, if she'd have the courage to call out for help. She tried to gather her thoughts, but being so consumed by terror and confusion, she was unable to. All she could do was keep hoping that he wanted nothing more than to take her money and that he'd leave her unharmed.

He hurriedly pushed her across the packed dirt and scattered gravel that led to the back of the hospital. The chain-link fence that surrounded the ruin had fallen into disrepair, and although it kept out most of the curious viewers, it was hardly a deterrent to anybody who was set on getting a closer look. The man quickly reached out with his free hand and pulled a section of the fence away. Pushing Jacey through the opening, he dragged her into the building to an area where portions of the remaining inner stone walls were still standing.

She was just about to beg him again to take her money and not hurt her when he spun her halfway around. Using his inner foot, he swept her ankle out from under her. The force of the blow sent her airborne for a split second before she fell to the ground, winding up facedown. The fall was painful, but she hadn't lost consciousness. With a chuckle, he placed his foot on the back of her neck. It was then that Jacey knew he had no intention of allowing her to live.

"Don't forget what I told you about screaming," he said, reaching down and clutching her forearm. While he dug his fingernails deep into the soft tissues of her arm and yanked her up, Jacey had the few seconds she needed to reach into her pocket, grab the pepper spray, and conceal it in her fisted hand.

Once he'd fully dragged her to her feet, he shifted his hand from her arm to her throat. Using his thumb and index finger like a pincer, he squeezed down on her windpipe. The pure force of his deadly stranglehold not only robbed her of oxygen but made it impossible for her to scream. He held her close with his other arm, but that meant his body was blocking his view of her hand. She wasted no time in seizing the opportunity. With one rapid motion, she yanked her hand up and unleashed the caustic spray directly in his face. With an anguished scream, he jerked his head back and released his grip. Rubbing his eyes madly, he backpedaled several feet.

Jacey's first instinct was to run, but he was blocking her only way to escape the room. Jacey watched as he continued to jerk his head wildly from side to side as he struggled to open his eyes. Her eyes flashed in every direction, but she couldn't see where his gun had landed. She spotted a broken segment of a two-by-four on the ground. She reached for the piece of lumber and picked it up. The moment she secured it in her hand, the man lurched forward. His arms were flailing uncontrollably, and Jacey could see his eyes were still tightly closed. He screamed as he swung his hands frantically in the air, trying to recapture her.

Somehow, he sensed her presence and turned sharply toward her and again sprang forward. Jacey's response was more instinctual than anything else. She took a quick step to the side, raised the two-by-four, spun her shoulders, and swung it low toward him, as hard as she was able. Her timing and aim were perfect. The wooden plank cut directly above his right ankle, sweeping the leg out from under him and sending him whirling out of control on his remaining leg. It seemed like a split-second later to Jacey that the man completely lost his balance, toppled forward, and collided head-first with a time-beaten, partially collapsed stone wall.

From the powerful blow to his head and chest, his legs folded and he crumbled to the ground. Blood poured from a deep jagged gash to his head and quickly welled up on the ground around his head and neck. The force of his weight slamming into the unstable wall sent several of the top stones tumbling to the ground. Jacey reacted by quickly stepping as far back from the wall as she could. The man didn't move, nor did he utter a sound. Jacey tried to see if he was breathing, but she couldn't be sure.

Before she could figure out her next step, a deafening sound of rumbling stones was followed by the entire wall crashing down, sending a dense mixture of sand and dirt spewing into the air. The man was left buried under an avalanche of stones. The only parts of him she could make out were his bloodied face, the side of his head, and the top of one twisted shoulder. Jacey stood motionless. She didn't scream. No professional oath she'd ever taken or tenet of medical ethics she embraced prompted her in any way to help him. To the contrary, she hoped he was dead.

Her mind suddenly shifted back to the realities of the here and now. Only caring about getting out of the building and finding help as fast as she was able, she turned and hurried outside. The instant she was beyond the fence and back onto the running trail, she broke into a frantic dash that took her fleeing from the skeletal remains of the smallpox hospital back toward the tram station.

FORTY-THREE

In spite of being breathless from running so hard, Jacey continued to race toward the Visitor Center. When she finally spotted a few people in the distance, she cried out for help. Two women responded immediately and helped her to a bench; a third called 911. A few moments later, a man walking his German shepherd appeared and identified himself as a nurse. He took off his lightweight ski jacket and draped it across her shoulders.

"You're safe now," one of the women told her, sitting down next to her and putting her arm around her. "The police and paramedics are on their way."

"Thank you," Jacey said. But in spite of her reassurances, Jacey couldn't stop shaking. The front of her neck ached from where the man had choked her, conjuring up the image of his terrifying face in her mind and reminding her that she'd come within inches of losing her life.

It didn't take long for a large group of curious onlookers to gather. As soon as two paramedics and a police officer arrived, the crowd went mute. When Jacey looked up and saw them, she finally began to feel she was out of immediate danger. But she struggled to collect herself enough to respond to the barrage of questions being leveled at her by the police officer and the paramedics.

When the questions stopped, she shifted her gaze out across the river toward Manhattan. Without consciously trying, her mind took her to a place where all the grating voices and raucous sounds of her surroundings faded to a palpable hush. She almost felt as if she'd become one of the observers instead of the victim.

The paramedics continued to work quickly to move her onto a stretcher. It was when they started to wheel her toward their truck that the events of the last hour finally caused her to burst into a deluge of tears.

· ·

With his weapon drawn, Bob DiMuro, an eleven-year veteran of the Roosevelt Island Public Safety Department, pushed past the chain-link fence and entered the Renwick Ruin. It took him only a minute to find the collapsed wall and see the man partially buried beneath it. He quickly scanned the area and saw the handgun about ten feet away before turning back to the man. In spite of the spilled stones, DiMuro could still see the man's face. His eyes were frozen open, fixed, and hollow. With no blood flow to his face, his skin was a pallid shade of gray. DiMuro could see enough of his torso to know he wasn't breathing. There was no question in his mind the man was dead.

He was just about to reach for his two-way radio when he noticed a bulge in the pouch-pocket of the man's hoodie. Thinking it could possibly be a second handgun, he reached his hand inside. But what he removed wasn't a weapon of any type— it was a black New York Yankees baseball cap.

FORTY-FOUR

Dr. Sean Weathers was just beginning another in a long series of busy emergency room shifts he'd been working for the past month. One of the patients assigned to him was a young woman who'd been the victim of a mugging. Caring for people who had been the target of a violent crime had become a scenario he was all too familiar with.

Having placed Dr. Jacey Flanigan high on his priority list, Sean took a few minutes to review the intake information gathered by the triage nurse.

"Good evening, Dr. Flanigan. My name's Sean Weathers. I'll be looking after you this evening. I'm very sorry for what happened to you. How are you doing?" he asked, as he approached the bed and began studying the bruises on her neck.

"Actually, from a physical-injury standpoint, I think I'm okay."

"Any trouble breathing, swallowing, or moving your neck?"

"No. I'm fine."

"Any numbness or weakness in your arms or hands?"

"No. My neck's a little sore, but I don't think I fractured a vertebra or suffered any nerve damage."

Continuing to check her, he said, "It sounds like you've already examined yourself. I'm starting to wonder what I'm doing here."

"Sorry," she said. "I guess it's hard to shift from doctor to patient."

"I take care of a lot of physicians. You're not alone in that challenge. Do you recall if you hit your head?"

"I don't think so."

"So, no loss of consciousness?"

"No."

"And your recollection of the events?"

"Unfortunately, perfect."

"You have some road rash on your back, but it's not too severe. The nurse will clean the area for you." She could feel his hands checking each of the bones of her back. "I think, to be on the safe side, we should get a few plain x-rays and a CT scan of your neck and back, and also check a few blood tests."

"If everything's okay afterward, I'd like to go home."

"Let's talk about that after we have the results of the tests. I'll be back as soon as I have them," he said, walking toward the door.

A few minutes later, one of the nurses came in to draw Jacey's blood. As soon as he was done, the transportation assistant arrived and took her to the CT scan suite. Thirty minutes later, the same assistant wheeled her back to her room.

Fatigue was starting to overcome her, and she closed her eyes. The next thing she knew, she was being awakened by Dr. Weathers coming back into the room.

"Well, other than some bruising to the soft tissues of your neck, you don't have any serious injuries. As far as your back goes, you just need some local care to deal with the minor cuts and abrasions. I think it's safe for you to go home."

"I'd prefer that, and thank you very much."

"In that case, I'll get going on the discharge paperwork." He started to turn toward the door, but then stopped. "I think you may already know this, but the asshole who attacked you is dead. I thought you might want to know."

"Thanks, but I still think it'll be a while before I'm totally comfortable setting foot outside my apartment."

"Do you live alone?"

"Yes."

"It might be a good idea to call a friend or relative. Maybe you shouldn't be alone tonight."

"Thanks."

"I'm sure the police are going to want to ask you a million more questions before you leave. They're waiting outside."

"That's okay. I kind of expected it."

"I'll be here until tomorrow morning. If you need anything, give me a call."

"Thanks again for your help."

Jacey had done her best to put on a good front for Sean and not giving him the impression she was on the verge of an emotional breakdown. She'd been shaken to her core with fear, and she was emotionally exhausted from her ordeal. With everything else that was going on at the hospital, she couldn't help but wonder how she'd hold up psychologically in the days and weeks to come.

FORTY-FIVE

When Jacey heard the doors open, she assumed it was the nurse returning with her discharge instructions or the police, but when she looked up, she was beyond surprised to see Nathan Beyer and Alexa Delacour.

Alexa was the first to speak. "Are you okay? Nathan called me when he heard what happened."

"My God, Jacey. I can't believe this happened to you," he said, walking up to stand at her bedside.

"I'm okay. I was very lucky."

"I love Manhattan," Alexa said, "but sometimes I really hate living here. Did all your tests and x-rays come back negative?"

"They did a CT of my back and neck. They were both negative."

"That's a blessing," Beyer said. "Are they admitting you to the hospital?"

"They gave me a choice, but I think I'd prefer to go home."

"Are you sure that's wise?" he asked.

"I'll be fine. I just need to get home."

"We'll arrange for a car to take you," Alexa said.

"That's very kind, but—"

"Let's not argue about it," Beyer was quick to insist. "And I'm expecting that you take as much time off as you need."

"Actually, I was just thinking about that, and I think the best thing for me is to get back to work as soon as possible. I'd rather be busy taking care of patients than thinking about what happened."

"We'll leave that entirely up to you, but just remember you have carte blanche to take as much time as you think you need."

"You may feel a lot more sore in the morning," Alexa said. "Why don't you wait until tomorrow before making a final decision about coming back to work so soon?"

Before Jacey could respond, the nurse walked into the room.

"Well, I guess we should get going," Beyer said, reaching into his coat pocket to pull out his phone. "I'll arrange for the car right now."

"Are you sure there's nothing we can do?" Alexa asked. "If you'd like, one of us can ride home with you."

"That won't be necessary, but thank you both for your concern. I can't tell you how much it means to me that you came to see me."

"Remember what I said about taking as much time as you need," Beyer said, as he and Alexa walked toward the door.

As soon as they were out of the room, the nurse finished treating the bruises and scrapes on her back. Jacey's mind was too numb to dwell on the attack any further, and at least for the moment, the only thing she cared about was getting out of the emergency room and home to her apartment.

FORTY-SIX

The moment Jacey arrived home, she double-locked the front door and went into the kitchen to pour herself a glass of cold sweet tea. The thought of calling her father and sister to tell them what happened crossed her mind, but after giving it some more thought, she decided to wait a day or two.

She turned on the television and sat down at the kitchen table. She tried but was unable to shake the vivid images from her mind of the man's face when he had his death-grip on her throat. On her way home from the hospital, she had hoped that more time and the confirmation that her assailant was dead would help put her mind at ease. But her hope was more imagined than real, and as she fought to concentrate on the television, her stomach tightened and churned with unrelenting fear.

Coaxing herself to breathe more deliberately, she kept repeating to herself that she was safe. But nothing helped, and she felt herself becoming more untethered from rational thought with each passing minute. Consumed with apprehension that she'd never be able to put her horrific experience behind her, she felt every inch of herself begin to shudder. Her hands trembled while all the muscles in her body tightened into a painful spasm. The only thing she could think to do, short of returning to the hospital, was to call her father. She was just about to get up to call him, when her phone rang.

It was Liam.

"Hello," she said.

"I was at the hospital and heard what happened. I'm sorry for calling you at home, but I just wanted to make sure you were okay."

"I guess I'm doing okay," she said, battling to sound in control, but doubting she'd pulled it off.

"Is there anything you need . . . or is there anything at all I can do for you?"

"Not right now," she answered, feeling herself fighting back a renewed wave of tears.

"Are you sure?"

A few seconds passed. Finally she said, in a voice drenched in desperation, "There is something you could do for me. Do you think you come over here and sit with me for a while?"

PART
T W O

Trial by Fire

FORTY-SEVEN

THREE WEEKS LATER
MONDAY

Fortunately, Jacey had no lasting physical injuries from being assaulted, and with each passing day, she felt emotionally and physically stronger and better able to stay focused on her patient responsibilities. In spite of the urging of Nathan Beyer, she had only taken a week off from work after the attack. She'd met with the police on several occasions. They finally informed her that the man who attacked her had a long history of violent crimes, and since they were convinced he'd acted alone, the investigation had been closed. The part of Jacey that was looking for closure didn't object to their decision not to pursue the matter. There were, however, other matters—those concerning patient care at MCHH—that continued to plague her.

Jacey and Liam had just finished making morning rounds and were about to take a short coffee break when her hospital phone rang.

"This is Dr. Flanigan."

"Good morning, Doctor. This is Marcy in Dr. Beyer's office. He was hoping you had a few minutes to stop by and speak with him."

"Of course," she said, "I'll be right there."

"Thank you. I'll let him know you're on your way."

Jacey appreciated Dr. Beyer's continued concern about her well-being. He'd called her every day to make certain she was getting along okay. He had also made arrangements for her to meet with a psychologist. Jacey would have probably declined his offer, but because he was so insistent, she took the path of least resistance and agreed to the session.

"Dr. Beyer wants to see me," she said to Liam. "I'll call you when I'm done. We can meet at the coffee bar and go over today's admissions."

"I'll be there."

Jacey went directly to the medical office building. As soon as she walked into Dr. Beyer's outer office, Marcy looked up from her computer screen and smiled.

"Go right in. He's waiting for you."

"Thanks."

Jacey knocked on his door and slowly opened it. The moment he looked up and saw her, he came out from behind his desk and met her in the middle of the room.

"Jacey, it's nice to see you. Please have a seat," he said, escorting her to a small conference table. "How are you feeling?"

"I'm fine. Getting back to work was the best thing for me."

"That's wonderful to hear." She wasn't sure why, but from the uneasy look on his face, she suspected he had something on his mind other than checking to see how she was doing.

"How did that session with Dr. Lam go?" he asked, fidgeting with his bowtie.

"Very well."

"Did you schedule another session?"

"No. She thought I was doing well enough under the circumstances and told me to call her if I felt the need to talk again."

"That's excellent." After a nervous hand steeple and clearing his throat, he went on, "I'm afraid there's a problem. I know this couldn't come at a worse time, but I have to discuss a very serious patient situation with you that was brought to my attention."

"Of course."

"Last week you saw a four-year-old boy in the post-op clinic. He had a VSD repair three months ago. His name's Bradley Sims."

"I remember him."

"Good. Well, then I'm sure you recall that Bradley's been having a lot of trouble with his teeth and needs several extractions. The procedure's scheduled for later this week."

"Yes, his father told me about it. Is there a problem?"

"His VSD repair required the placement of an artificial patch to close the hole, which means there would be a strict requirement that he receive protective antibiotics before his dental procedure to prevent a life-threatening heart infection." Since the need for antibiotics was something a third-year medical student would be expected to know, Jacey was perplexed why Dr. Beyer would even mention it to her.

Still uncertain where he was going with all this, she stated plainly, "I'm well aware of the necessity. That's why I prescribed an antibiotic to be given by the parents before the dental procedure."

"I'm afraid that's the problem," Beyer said, with the discomfort in his voice increasing with every word he uttered. "Did you remember to make a note of it in Bradley's chart?"

"Of course. Everything I just told you is well documented in my clinic visit note."

"This is very awkward, but we checked his chart, and we can't seem to find your note. I have to ask you again—is there any chance you forgot to write one?"

"Of course not, Dr. Beyer."

"Well, we asked the IT Department to get involved, and even they can't locate it. And, to make matters worse, Bradley's father's absolutely adamant that you never told him about the necessity for antibiotics."

Jacey practically jumped to her feet.

"That's absurd. Of course I told him. And how could a note just disappear from a patient's medical record? What you're telling me is impossible."

"All evidence to the contrary. At least for the moment," Beyer informed her. "Fortunately, one of the nurses noticed the omission and brought it to our attention. We were able to contact Mr. Sims and make sure Bradley got his antibiotic prescription."

"This is ridiculous. I prescribed the antibiotic. I even asked Mr. Sims if he wanted me to send it electronically to his pharmacy. He told me he'd rather have a handwritten prescription. I wrote it out myself and handed it to him with very specific instructions when it should be given. I documented everything in the chart," she stated emphatically.

"Well, technology's not my strong suit, but I can assure you there's no note in his chart. The IT Department even checked the charts of every child you saw in the clinic that day, thinking you might have accidently put Bradley's note in one of theirs," he explained, shaking his head slowly. "You're of course free to check on all of this yourself."

"Rest assured, I will."

"Unfortunately . . . and to nobody's surprise, the cardiac surgeons are in an uproar about this. They insist you made an egregious and unforgiveable mistake in the care of one of their patients. They're accusing you of negligence and malfeasance and insisting you appear in front of the Peer Review Committee to explain your care of this child."

"Which means what, exactly?" Jacey's level of professionalism was rapidly being eroded by her rising indignation. Being accused of incompetence was not something she had much experience in dealing with.

"The committee will consider if you provided substandard care to Bradley. If they decide you did, they'll make corrective active recommendations. Unfortunately, they have far-reaching authority regarding issues of physician competency and behavior."

"But you said the problem was discovered and rectified. Bradley got a prescription for antibiotics, which means my alleged error had no adverse effect on the patient."

"Not this time."

"Excuse me?"

"The point is, whether the patient suffered an injury as a result of negligent care really isn't the core issue." Beyer again paused, this time drumming the table. "I'm afraid there are several other issues regarding your performance and professional behavior which have also been raised." He paused, sighed, and with averted eyes, added, "The surgeons want those discussed as well, and I'm afraid Dr. Gault agrees."

"Dr. Gault? What's he got to do with this?"

"He's the Chair of the Peer Oversight Committee. He's the one who's insisting the committee be convened as soon as possible to address the entire matter."

Jacey's heart almost dropped a beat. She pushed her palms together and asked, "When?"

"This Friday morning at eight thirty."

"They can't be serious. That's four days from now. That doesn't give me enough time to prepare."

"I raised the same objection."

"And?"

"Dr. Gault doesn't feel you need time to prepare. He insists that all you have to do is simply answer the committee's questions truthfully. And since he's the chairman, it's within his purview to set the meeting whenever he pleases."

"Am I at least allowed to know the other areas the surgeons are so concerned about?"

Beyer stood, reached for a folder on his desk, and handed it to Jacey.

"It's all in the file," he said, again sitting at the table. "But to begin with, there are those two major altercations you had with Dr. Gault."

"Two physicians have a couple of disagreements. It happens. I hardly think that's reason enough to drag me in front of a disciplinary committee."

"Dr. Gault's accused you of unprofessional conduct. In his opinion, your behavior was sufficiently improper to require your presence before the committee."

"If we're talking about improper and unprofessional behavior, at least we've hit on a topic he's got plenty of experience with," Jacey was quick to announce.

"As I said, he chairs the committee, and . . . well, he can do pretty much as he pleases."

"With all due respect, that hardly sounds fair."

"Fair is like beauty—it's in the eye of the beholder."

"For goodness' sake, can't you see they're setting me up?"

"For what reason?"

"To get rid of me."

Nathan sighed, interlocked his fingers, and responded, "I think you're overreacting, Jacey."

"My God," she muttered to herself. She could plainly see she was shouting at the rain. Based on Dr. Beyer's prior unsupportive behavior, she doubted he'd have the backbone to stand behind her this time. She quickly realized that persisting in defending herself was a waste of time. "Does the committee have any other matters of concern that I'll have to answer for?"

He drew out a paper from the file folder Jacey had laid on the table. "They've been advised that you conducted at least two research chart reviews without first obtaining the approval of the IRB Committee. Such unofficial reviews are strictly prohibited by the hospital's bylaws." He lowered the paper and looked at her over the top of his reading glasses. "Did you really do that without permission?"

"Yes."

"For God's sake, Jacey. Why in the world would you do that?"

"Suffice it say, I had a good reason."

"I'm not sure that type of response will be viewed as reasonable justification for your decision to ignore a strict hospital policy." He cleared his throat, moved back in his chair, and continued, "It was also reported that you were in the Research Center in the middle of the night, sitting in a dark lab, pretending to be working at a microscope." He took his glasses off and tossed them on the table. "Is that true as well?"

"Yes."

"I'd ask you why, but I don't think you'd tell me. And, finally, there's the matter of the unorthodox request you made to one of the pharmacists. You're not obligated to discuss any of these matters with me, but I'm certainly happy to listen as a trusted friend and mentor, if you'd like."

"I appreciate your offer, but I'm not sure what to do at this point, so I think I'd prefer to say nothing."

"Well, you haven't been suspended, so until the meeting on Friday, it's business as usual with respect to your clinical responsibilities." He sighed, and with an appeasing smile, said, "In spite of what you may think, the committee members are reasonable people. I'm sure if you can present sound explanations for your actions, their response will be . . . well, proportional to your errors in judgment and the way you handle yourself."

Even though she suspected it was a rhetorical question, she asked, "What's the worst thing that can happen to me?"

"Well, if they should decide to revoke your hospital privileges, you'd be forbidden from practicing medicine at MCHH. According to your contract with our group, you'd be subject to immediate termination. And by law, the hospital would be required to report the incident to the state medical board."

"Do you think all of that's likely to happen?" she asked in a monotone.

"I think a lot of that will depend upon your attitude and how you present yourself in front of the committee. If you're contrite and forthcoming, I expect you may come out of this okay. If not, I expect the committee will recommend severe corrective action."

"I see," Jacey said, watching Beyer stand up and walk over to a dark wood bookcase.

"What I'm trying to say, Jacey, is your future at MCHH is in your hands. The committee members are aware of what happened to you. They know Bradley's clinic visit came at a time when you had just returned to work after a very traumatic event. As far as the other issues, I would apologize and assure the committee members that there will be major changes in your behavior, moving forward."

Jacey had always known who she was. Groveling had never been part of her DNA and she didn't see that changing now to protect her job. She stood up and headed toward the door.

"Thank you for the advice," she said, absent so much as a backward glance. "I'll give it serious consideration."

Instead of feeling panic or dread, Jacey could feel herself filling with sheer resolve. If the powers that be at MCHH wanted to say when this sham of a procedure was to begin, she'd do everything in her power to say when it was over. Her days of being an easy target for bullying "superiors" were over.

FORTY-EIGHT

As had become her custom, Jacey's first stop on morning rounds was to see Marc. Intent on putting her hospital-politics problems aside while she saw her patients, she spent an hour going over every detail of his condition. When she was finished, she prepared herself to make another difficult morning call to Laine to inform her that although Marc was stable, he was still showing no signs of emerging from his coma. Jacey tried her best to paint a guarded but hopeful picture, but it became more obvious every day that Laine was holding onto the bottom rung of her ladder.

After leaving the ICU, Jacey walked over to the post-op unit to meet Liam and check on how their patients had fared overnight. She hoped to be able to clear her afternoon schedule to give her the opportunity to start working on her defense in anticipation of her appearance in front of the Oversight Committee.

The moment she walked onto the unit, she spotted Andrea walking toward her.

"How are you?" Andrea asked, with a knowing glance.

Jacey grinned and shook her head. "From that look on your face, you've obviously already heard."

"I'm afraid so. Bad news and juicy gossip spread like a brush-fire in a stiff breeze around here. What are you going to do?"

"I've been asking myself that same question ever since I walked out of Dr. Beyer's office yesterday," she told her, in no mood at the moment to discuss the details of her problem or what she planned to do about it.

"I'm not going to say I told you so, but I—"

"You just did."

"Sorry. So, how do you plan to handle this mess?"

"Ask me that again tonight. I'm still gathering my thoughts."

"Did Dr. Beyer offer you the 'deal'?" Andrea asked, forming her fingers into air quotes.

"The deal?"

"It's the hospital's standard way of painlessly parting ways with those higher-ranking individuals who've fallen short of their expectations in either attitude or performance. In your case, you'd quietly resign your position, and magically, this entire disaster goes away. There will be no meeting of the Peer Oversight Committee, no suspension of your hospital privileges, and no written record in your file of anything that occurred. But most importantly, nothing will be reported to the state medical board, which is the last thing you want."

"That all sounds very neat and expedient, except for one minor problem—I've done nothing that warrants resigning. It's also the cowardly way out."

"For God's sake, Jacey, you're a pediatric cardiologist. Assuming your record's clean, you can get another job in a heartbeat anywhere in the country. But all that changes if the hospital and medical board decide to get nasty."

"So, being the victim of a gross injustice and deliberately ignoring possible substandard medical practices to save my job . . . that's okay? That's what you're suggesting?"

"Key word: *possible* substandard medical practices," Andrea said, moving a step closer as she spoke. "Tell me, Jacey, are you looking for justice, or to save your career? Nobody's going to hire you without speaking to the bigwigs here at MCHH. If you don't play ball, they'll trash you at every children's hospital in the country."

Jacey folded her arms in front of her. "I gave Bradley's father an antibiotic prescription and told him how important it was that his son receive the medication before the dental procedure. I know it, he knows it, and I suspect the jerks who are dragging me in front of the committee also know it. I appreciate your advice, but I'm not going to be the victim of some sick, twisted farce of a hearing. If I do what you suggest, I'll never be able to live with myself."

"The word is that Bradley's father backed the hospital."

"What a surprise. In case you don't know it, I've been prohibited by the hospital's attorney from contacting Mr. Sims directly. With that stop sign, I have no way of knowing where he truly stands."

"C'mon, Jacey. You sound like you believe you've been the victim of some premeditated conspiracy."

"I guess I'm not making myself clear, because that's *precisely* how I feel. I know I'm telling the truth. I guess it's up to you to decide who you want to believe." Jacey knew instantly she'd said the wrong thing. "Sorry, I shouldn't be directing my anger your way. You've been a great friend."

"Don't worry about it."

"Look Andrea, even if they offer me the *deal*, as you put it, I'd never take it. It's beneath me."

"I understand."

"I guess I'm under more stress than I realized. Look, I should finish rounds. What do you say we talk about all of this later?"

"Sure. Just give me a call."

Jacey stood at the core desk and watched Andrea disappear down the hall. She decided her schedule for the day had just changed. She reached for her phone and told Liam she'd be tied up for the next few hours and that she'd call him when she was ready to start rounds.

As soon as she was off the phone, she walked off the unit and went straight to her office. After sitting down at her desk and taking a moment to mentally steady herself, she reached for a white legal pad and picked up the antique-style fountain pen her father had given her the day she graduated from college. She knew she had a lot of ground to cover and very little time to do it before Friday.

Amidst a great deal of uncertainty, Jacey was sure about one thing—knowing exactly where she'd begin.

FORTY-NINE

Jacey wasted no time bringing up the website of Medicept Solutions, MCHH's provider for their electronic medical record system. The corporation was one of the largest developers of hospital-based computer systems in the country. Because it was the same system Jacey had used at Montana Children's, she was quite adept and familiar with it.

As soon as she located their phone number, she called and used the automated directory to reach Dr. Chris Silva's office.

"This is Chris Silva."

"Hi, Chris. This is Jacey Flanigan calling," she said, relieved she hadn't gotten his voice mail. "You may not remember me, but a couple of years ago I was one of the Medicept coaches at—"

"Montana Children's. Of course I remember you. You were one of the best coaches we ever worked with. You were a huge help when we rolled out our upgraded system."

"Thanks."

"Are you still in Montana?"

"No. I finished my training there and took a job in New York at Manhattan Children's Heart Center."

"That's a great hospital, and one of our biggest clients. I spent three months there a few years ago when they converted to our system. What can I do for you?"

"I have a problem I was hoping you could help me with."

"Shoot."

"A few days ago, I wrote a standard clinic note on a patient, which, for reasons that I can't understand, has completely disappeared from the chart. I've done everything I can think of to restore it, but nothing's worked. I was hoping you might have some tips to help me locate it."

"Sure, I'm happy to help. Let's start with the most obvious—and I know you've thought about this, but is it possible you accidently wrote the note on the wrong patient?"

"Not a chance."

"Do you remember if the system went down that day or if there were any significant upgrades going on?"

"I checked that. There definitely weren't any."

Chris then spent the next half hour walking Jacey through the standard steps of recovering a lost note. Most of them were techniques she was familiar with and had already attempted.

"Based on what you're telling me and what we've tried, it's going to be tough to restore the note," he said.

"Tough or impossible?"

"Nothing's impossible when it comes to our system," he proclaimed proudly. "MCHH has a tech support contract with us. There are some other things I can try on my own from here if you'd like."

"I'd really appreciate that."

"If you don't mind me saying so, you sound a little stressed out by this."

"Let's just say, it's very important I find that note."

"I'll give it my best shot, Jacey, but it may take me a couple of days to see if I can do anything. I'll call you either way."

"Thanks, Chris. I really appreciate your assistance."

"I gathered that," he told her.

Seeing as she was working on a tight time limit, Jacey ended the call with Chris only slightly optimistic that he'd be able to find Bradley's note in time for the committee meeting.

FIFTY

Jacey finished making some notes on her conversation with Chris before turning her attention to the next call she wanted to make. She pulled up Annalise Meehan's chart, located the phone number of her referring physician, and made the call.

"Dr. Snyder's office, this is Randy. How may I help you?"

"This is Dr. Flanigan calling from Manhattan Children's Heart. Would it be possible to speak with Dr. Snyder regarding Annalise Meehan?"

"Of course, we know her well. I'll tell the doctor you're on the phone. Please hold."

After a moment, Jacey heard, "This is Dr. Snyder."

"Good morning. My name's Jacey Flanigan. I'm one of the cardiologists at Manhattan Children's Heart. The reason for my call is to see if you have any questions regarding the care Annalise Meehan's received here, and to let you know how much we appreciate you referring her to us for surgery."

"Thank you, and as much as I appreciate your call, I'm afraid I wasn't the one who referred her to you."

"I'm—I'm surprised to hear that. The parents listed you as the referring physician, and we have a written report from you briefing us on her condition."

"There must be some mistake. I'm Annalise's pediatrician, but I never sent a letter of referral. I've taken care of her since the Meehans adopted her as a baby. She's always been in perfect health. I've listened to her heart a dozen times, and I've never heard a murmur, so when I heard she had a VSD diagnosed and then repaired in New York, I was quite surprised, to say the least."

"So, in all the time you've cared for her, she never had any weight loss, fatigue, shortness of breath . . . those types of symptoms?"

"Never," he answered. "I may not be practicing big-city pediatrics, but I'd like to think I've been around long enough not to miss a major congenital heart defect like a VSD. I'm sorry, Dr. Flanigan, but I didn't know a thing about Annalise's VSD or her undergoing surgery until very recently, when her parents brought her in and told me about it. If anybody had asked me a month ago, I would have said she was one of the healthiest kids in my practice."

Beyond perplexed, Jacey asked, "Did the Meehans mention the circumstances surrounding her transfer to our hospital?"

"They told me they were visiting relatives in upstate New York when Annalise became seriously ill. They took her to the local emergency room, and it was the doctor there who arranged the urgent transfer to MCHH."

"I apologize for the confusion, Dr. Snyder. I'll recheck Annalise's chart. I've made dozens of phone calls to our referring pediatricians in the last few days. I must have her confused with another patient."

"Not a problem. You sound fairly young. It'll happen more as you get older," he joked.

Jacey forced a polite chuckle. "If you don't mind, I may call you back when I have all of this straightened out."

"I'm fine with that. Have a nice day."

Even though she was seated, Jacey felt her feet slowly begin to shuffle beneath her desk. It was a subconscious habit she'd developed as a child when faced with a confusing situation. She had no reason to suspect the accuracy of Dr. Snyder's accounting of Annalise's illness. The problem was that she'd been over her chart several times and was certain there was no referral note or any other medical records from an emergency room in New York. She could think of no logical reason for their absence.

First it was Bradley Sim's clinic note that mysteriously disappeared, and now, an entire transfer record had gone missing. The sophistication and reliability of MCHH's electronic medical record systems argued against a technical error of some type. It seemed the inexplicable problem of disappearing medical records at MCHH was becoming epidemic in the Cardiac Surgery Division.

Jacey remained lost in thought for another few minutes. Finally, she reached for her phone and called Roxanna McArdle, her practice coordinator. Roxanna was highly organized and efficient but at times lacked a filter between what popped into her head and what came out of her mouth.

"Hi Roxanna, I have some post-op VSD patients I want to bring into the clinic for a routine follow-up exam and an ultrasound. If I get you a list, can you set up the appointments?"

"Sure. How many and what's the timeframe?"

"I'd say around seven patients. I was hoping to get them in by Thursday at the latest."

"This Thursday? All of them?"

"I'm afraid so."

"I haven't worked with you that long, but you seem to have a method to your madness, so as soon as you send me the list, I'll do my best to set up the appointments."

"Thanks, and I'd prefer if you didn't discuss these visits with anybody."

"What visits?"

"Thanks. I'll explain later."

"Not necessary," Roxanna replied.

Unable to shake her conversation with Dr. Snyder from her mind, Jacey pushed back in her chair and closed her eyes.

She realized she was again embarking on behavior that would ruffle the feathers of the heart surgeons. But based on the way she'd been treated, whether they found out about the visits or not was a matter of complete indifference to her. Whatever concerns she'd had about adapting to hospital politics had evaporated the moment Dr. Beyer informed her the surgeons were behind her having to appear in front of the Peer Oversight Committee. While Dr. Beyer may have seen it as a necessary hospital procedure, Jacey viewed it as an unjustifiable humiliation.

FIFTY-ONE

Jacey didn't finish seeing her last patient until at a few minutes before six. With a lot on her mind, she decided to have dinner at a small French brasserie she discovered when she first interviewed at MCHH. It was less than a two-block walk from the hospital, and she enjoyed the relaxed atmosphere and had fallen in love with their shrimp-and-lobster rolls.

She was waiting to pay the check when her phone rang. She checked the caller ID but didn't recognize the number.

"Hello, this is Jacey Flanigan."

"Dr. Flanigan, my name's Mary Laraby. I'm Mitch's mother. I was hoping you'd have a minute to talk with me."

"Of course, Mrs. Laraby. I was so sorry to learn of Mitch's death. I just recently started working at the hospital. Mitch went out of his way to make me feel welcome."

"That sounds like him and that's kind of you to say. I should begin by apologizing for calling you on your cellphone. Andrea and Mitch were good friends, and she gave it to me. She assured me you wouldn't mind."

"It's fine. You're welcome to call me any time."

"Thank you. I'll get right to the point. I was going through some of Mitch's personal effects and came across a file with your name on it. I thought maybe you two were working on a project together. I mentioned it in passing to Andrea, who suggested I call you. I was hoping we could meet so that I could give it to you."

"Certainly. When would be a good time for you?"

"Actually, I came over to the hospital on another matter concerning Mitch. I brought the file with me, hoping you'd still be here. I'm right outside the main entrance."

"I'm not in the hospital, but I'm only a couple of blocks away and I was just about to head back. If you're able to wait a few minutes, I'd be happy meet you right now."

"That's not a problem. It's a beautiful evening. I'll wait right here for you."

Jacey paid her check and started back toward the hospital. When she was approaching the main entrance, she spotted a petite, smartly dressed woman standing on the sidewalk with a large manila envelope in her hands.

"Mrs. Laraby?"

"Yes," she said, extending her hand with an inviting smile. "It's nice to meet you. And please call me Mary."

"The pleasure's mine. I again want to tell you how very saddened we all were to learn of Mitch's passing."

"It was a horrible accident. I miss him terribly. I lost my husband two years ago, so it's just me now," she said with a sober expression, as she handed Jacey the envelope. "Mitch spoke very highly of you. He wasn't the most complimentary of people, so I assume you must have really impressed him."

"That's very kind of you to say."

"If you'd like to take a look, I'm happy to wait."

Jacey opened the envelope and looked inside. From her brief view, the contents appeared to be a few dozen medical journal articles and several pages of handwritten notes inside a file folder.

"Do you have any idea why Mitch chose these articles?"

"I don't, but my son made no secret of the fact that he had serious concerns regarding the medical practices at MCHH. If I had to guess, I'd say this material is in some way related to those concerns," she answered. "Mitch was an extremely intelligent young man, Dr. Flanigan, and far too busy to waste his time chasing down half-baked theories." She paused to slip on a pair of brown leather gloves. "I would wager that the answers to your questions are in his notes."

"I'm going to review all of the material very carefully. I hope you're right."

"It was nice meeting you," Mitch's mother said, again extending a hand.

"Can I offer you a ride?"

"I don't live far, and actually, I'd prefer to walk," she answered, buttoning her coat all the way up.

As Mary Laraby walked away, Jacey's ride pulled up to the curb. The driver stepped out of the SUV and opened the door for her.

"Good evening, Dr. Flanigan," he said. "There's not too much traffic tonight. I should have you home in no time."

"Thank you," Jacey said, getting into the car.

More than a little anxious to get home and start poring over the contents of Mitch's file, she hoped her driver was right in his prediction.

FIFTY-TWO

Three hours after she'd arrived home, Jacey was still immersed in Mitch's journal articles and notes. For reasons she couldn't understand, he'd compiled a list of twenty-two children's hospitals. They were all well-known institutions and were located in and around Manhattan. She studied the list again, but nothing jumped out at her that would distinguish one from the next. Fatigued from her long day, Jacey decided to put her concerns to bed for the night and revisit the enigma of Mitch's file in the morning.

Sitting on the floor with her back against the couch with all of the material strewn out around her, she yawned and stretched her hands high over her head. As she started to pick it up to replace it in the file folder, it crossed her mind that it might help to simply hear a friendly voice. The choice of that someone was easy. She reached for her cell phone.

"Hi, Daddy. How are you feeling? How did the radiation therapy go?"

"It was a piece of cake. I'm fine," he answered, unconvincingly. "You usually don't call me until the weekend. What's going on?"

"I'm just trying to get ready for this meeting on Friday."

"You were a little unsure of your strategy when we spoke Monday evening."

"Other than being polite and professional and presenting the facts as they really are, I'm going to play it perfectly straight. I'm not going to allow them to provoke me in any way. Dr. Beyer told me that Gault insists there's nothing personal about any of this."

"To which you said . . ."

"I told him to tell Dr. Gault that it doesn't get any more personal than this."

"I would have handled it the same way."

"I'm glad to hear that. It makes me feel like I'm getting a little more savvy about things."

"Preparation is everything in these matters. Don't make any claims or conclusions you can't back up," he advised her, before adding, "It's a sad truth, but hospital politics can be more stressful than a lot of the diseases we treat."

"I'm learning that one the hard way. I'll give you a call tomorrow. I can't wait until this weekend. I love you, Daddy."

FIFTY-THREE

In spite of being thoroughly spent, Jacey was unable to fall asleep. She tried every mind trick she knew to help her drift off, but none worked. She was still debating the prospect of taking a pill when her phone rang.

"Jacey. It's Chris from Medicept. I'm sorry about the hour, but I know how anxious you are about your missing note. If this isn't a good time, I can call you tomorrow."

"No. Now's perfect. I was going to call you first thing in the morning," she said, pushing herself up and leaning back against the leather headboard. "I hope you're about to tell me you found my clinic note . . . ?"

"I'm afraid it's a little more complicated than that." There was a clear hesitancy in his voice, which made her hopes sink like a load of iron ore. She reached over and turned on her bedside lamp.

"Look, Jacey. It's not like you and I really know each other that well, so please forgive the question . . . but is everything okay in New York?"

"That probably depends on what you're going to tell me."

"I found your note, but I think there's something you should know."

As Chris began to explain what he'd discovered, Jacey found herself holding on to every word. With disbelief, she reached for the pen and legal pad she kept on her nightstand. After he'd explained his findings to her, he summed up by saying, "I can't say that I've ever seen anything like this. Does any of this make sense to you?"

"I really don't know. I think I need some time to digest all of this."

"There's one other thing. We have a contract with MCHH to troubleshoot any problems that come up with our system. As part of the process, I'm required to send in a written report of my finding to your IT Department."

Jacey was fighting back the uncertainty when she asked, "How much time can you give me?"

"I'm afraid Monday morning's the best I can do."

"That would help me."

"I was hoping it might."

"Thanks, Chris. I—I hardly know what to say."

"No problem," he assured her. "Is there anything else I can do?"

After gathering sufficient courage, Jacey said, "Well, at the risk of being even more pushy, there is this one other thing."

FIFTY-FOUR

With the Peer Oversight Committee meeting only one day away, Jacey felt like an overwound spring. Knowing she'd only get one chance to refute the allegations against her only fanned the flames of her apprehension. It even crossed her mind that the committee members had already made up their minds, and that her appearance was nothing more than a facade—a kangaroo court of sorts, whose only purpose was to provide Dr. Gault with the means he needed to ruin her career.

After a long day, she finished seeing the last of the seven patients who she'd asked Roxanna to schedule for clinic visits. She was sitting in her office reviewing their lab results when Andrea walked in.

"What are you doing here?" Jacey asked, with a curious grin. "Aren't you supposed to be in the hospital?"

"I heard you were over here. Since I know this isn't your normal clinic day and that you were probably up to something that would get your butt into even more hot water, I thought I'd stroll on over here to see if I could save you from yourself."

Jacey tried, but she couldn't contain a chuckle.

"Is there anything that goes on around here that you don't know about?"

"Not with the network of friends I've built up around here," Andrea said, taking a seat and putting her feet up on a small stepstool. "So, what are you doing?"

"The Peer Oversight Committee meeting's tomorrow. Every time I close my eyes, I hear this very loud ticking bomb. So, I thought I'd get my mind off things by coming over here and seeing a few extra patients."

"Seriously?"

"Seriously," Jacey repeated.

"What kind of extra patients?"

"Kurt and some other VSD repairs. I'm doing some follow-up ultrasounds."

"Since when did that become part of the post-op protocol? Once they have their ultrasound on the day of discharge, we don't do another one unless there's a reason."

"I'm starting a new protocol."

Andrea's chin dropped like a stone. She said, in a voice rich with sarcasm, "I see. And do the elite from the fourth floor know about this new protocol?"

"If you're referring to the heart surgeons, I didn't ask for their approval."

"Since we both know these visits today aren't a matter of routine, what are you looking for on these ultrasounds?"

"Nothing in particular. I'm just trying to be thorough," Jacey explained, having no interest in getting into a detailed conversation with Andrea about what she was really looking for.

"I better get back to the hospital. If, for some reason, you feel the need to speak to somebody, give me a call. Oh, I'm sure you already know this, but Jenna Gatewood was readmitted earlier today for surgery tomorrow. Her VSD repair's scheduled for one p.m."

"I was planning on seeing her as soon as I was finished over here."

"Good. Abby already asked me if you'd be in today."

"And you covered me by saying . . ."

"I told her that of course you'd be in today."

Jacey laughed. It was the first time she could remember doing so since hearing that she was being dragged in front of the Peer Oversight Committee. "Thanks," she said, as Andrea left the office.

A minute later, Danielle, the radiology technician who had performed all of the ultrasounds, tapped on the door and walked in.

"Have you had a chance to look at any of the studies yet?" she asked.

"I've been too busy just trying to write my notes and check the lab work. I was planning on having a look at them at home tonight."

"All seven ultrasounds are loaded into the computer, so you should be good to go whenever you want to look at them."

"Thanks. You're a lifesaver."

"Anytime, Dr. Flanigan. And good luck tomorrow," she said, holding up crossed fingers. She hesitated for a few seconds before going on, "I hope you know that you have a lot of fans around here, and we're all pulling for you. This place needs more doctors like you."

"Thanks, Danielle. That's an incredibly nice thing to say and couldn't have come at a better time."

"Call me if you have any questions about the ultrasounds."

Jacey reached for her phone and called Roxanna.

"How busy are you?"

"Things are pretty quiet. I was thinking of heading home, but something tells me that's not going to happen."

"I could use some help getting ready for tomorrow's meeting," Jacey said.

"Where do you want to meet?"

Thanking her lucky stars for Roxanna's willingness to help, Jacey answered, "How about my office in fifteen minutes. After we're done, I'll go see Jenna."

"See you there."

The sheer strain from the limited time Jacey had left to prepare for the committee meeting was taking a large toll on her. Almost from the minute she learned about her problem from Dr. Beyer, she'd been battling a painfully raw churning in the pit of her stomach. She wasn't a stranger to high-pressure timelines, but nothing she'd ever experienced compared to the unrelenting stress of trying to get ready for her appearance tomorrow.

She took a peek at the cheap digital clock on her desk. She closed her eyes and prayed she'd have enough time and smarts to build her case for tomorrow's meeting. If she failed, her future as a pediatric cardiologist might wind up the same way as skywriting on a windy day.

FIFTY-FIVE

After spending an hour with Roxanna and then checking in on Jenna, Jacey gathered her things and left the hospital. They'd made some progress, but she knew she still had a lot of work to do before the meeting. Bordering on desperate, Jacey resorted to groveling and somehow persuaded Roxanna to meet her at six in the morning to finish up the preparations.

When she was finished with dinner, Jacey made herself a mug of green tea and went into her living room. She found a spot in the corner of her lumpy couch, opened her laptop, and signed on to MCHH's medical records system. She started with a young boy named Luke Winslow and looked at the ultrasound images Danielle had done earlier.

After going through each image, Jacey looked away from her laptop screen and stared across the room at a watercolor of a tranquil cove tucked into the Maine coastline.

"This isn't possible," she muttered, as she looked back at her screen and checked the name and date on the ultrasound, just to make sure there hadn't been some mistake and she was looking at a different patient's ultrasound. But there was no mistake. It was definitely Luke's.

Still mystified, Jacey decided to move on to the next child's study. The patient was a three-year-old with a VSD, who Dr. Corbett had operated on nine months earlier. When Jacey saw the findings were identical to Luke's, she felt her throat stiffen.

Cautioning herself not to jump to conclusions, she carefully went through the remaining five ultrasounds of the patients she'd seen in clinic. When she was done, she sat on the couch, frozen somewhere between confused and dumbfounded.

Moving past her shock, she reached for her phone and dialed MCHH's Radiology Department.

"Radiology, this is Gina."

"Hi, Gina. It's Dr. Flanigan. Is Dr. Rayburn still in the department?"

"She sure is. We're having one of those nights, if you know what I mean."

"I'm sure I do. Can you please connect me to her?"

"Sure."

Jacey stood up and paced behind the coffee table while she waited for Bridgette Rayburn to answer her phone.

"This is Dr. Rayburn."

"Hi, Bridgette. It's Jacey Flanigan. I know this is going to sound a little crazy—and I heard how busy you are—but I was hoping you might be able to go over some ultrasounds with me."

"Now?"

"I know. And I'm sorry, but I really need your help."

"Okay, give me the patient's medical record numbers and I'll start pulling them up."

"Actually, I was kind of hoping we could do this in person. I'm at home, but I can grab a cab and meet you in the reading room in twenty minutes."

"Wow, this must be important."

"I wouldn't be asking if it weren't."

"C'mon over. You sound frantic. What's going on?"

"That's what you're going to help me figure out. I'll see you in twenty minutes."

With goosebumps running down her arms, Jacey grabbed her purse and dashed out of her apartment.

FIFTY-SIX

It was eight thirty when Jacey and Bridgette finished reviewing the ultrasounds.

After some reflection and an awkward silence, Jacey managed to gather her courage.

"If I need you tomorrow, will you help me?" she asked, feeling as if she was on the brink of losing it in front of a colleague.

"What choice do I have?"

"I didn't mean to sound like I'm pushing you into—"

"It's got nothing to do with that. If what you've uncovered is real—and I think it is—how could I refuse to help you bring it to light? I'd never be able to live with myself."

"Thanks, Bridgette," Jacey said, with a slow smile.

"I'll see you tomorrow," Bridgette promised, giving her a quick hug.

Jacey left the hospital, grabbed a cab, and was home in fifteen minutes. She was just pulling a bottle of iced tea from the refrigerator when her phone rang.

"How are you doing?" her father asked.

"I'm fine. What about you?"

"I'm doing well," he answered. "So, tomorrow's the big day. Are you ready?"

"I guess that remains to be seen. This is the most nervous I've ever felt in my life."

"Stay focused. Gault and the others may be important people in the hospital, but remember: an asshole's an asshole."

Jacey smiled broadly.

"Good luck tomorrow. I'm sure you'll kick their sorry butts around the block."

"I'll sure try."

"Don't forget to call me afterward."

"I won't, and thanks for the pep talk. Goodnight, Daddy."

Discouraged but giving no thought to giving up, Jacey tossed her phone on the couch. She was convinced there was a connection between what she'd discovered on the ultrasounds and Mitch's fears. But whatever that common thread was . . . it escaped her.

She spent another hour going through the all the articles and notes in Mitch's file. The last thing she looked at before she decided to call it a night was the list of children's hospitals he'd compiled and how it could possibly tie into the articles, which largely concerned themselves with the future financial landscape of medicine. The uncertainty of where medicine would be in the years to come occupied the time and energy of a great number of national experts in health care. Some used highly sophisticated projection models to predict the future, while others thought that was about as accurate and useful as reading tea leaves.

Feeling herself starting to nod off, Jacey put everything back in the file and tossed it on the coffee table. She covered an immense yawn with her palm and then stretched her arms. She pushed herself up and started to walk toward her bedroom.

She'd only taken a few steps when she turned and looked back at Mitch's file. All at once, the pieces of the enigma came together. It was if they had a mind of their own and had suddenly decided to reveal themselves to her. A pulse of adrenaline flowed through her veins, leaving her palms moist and her heart thumping like a jackhammer.

Jacey closed her eyes. She was annoyed at herself for being slow on the uptake, but her disappointment paled in comparison to her relief in finally knowing what had terrified Dr. Mitch Laraby.

PART
THREE

Good and Evil

FIFTY-SEVEN

When Jacey walked into her office at ten minutes to six and saw Roxanna already sitting at her desk waiting for her, she allowed a huge breath of relief to surge from her lungs. Even though Jacey had been up most of the night preparing for the meeting, she was bright-eyed and ready to work. For the next two-plus hours, Roxanna assisted her in putting the final touches on her presentation to the committee.

"Showtime's in twenty minutes," Roxanna said, tapping the crystal of her watch. "Is there anything else we need to do?"

"If I'm not ready now, I never will be," Jacey said, rolling her shoulders to ease her stressed muscles. "I wish I could find the words to thank you for all your help."

"No thanks necessary."

"You sound like my father. No matter how this comes out, the best dinner in the city's on me. You've earned it."

"I accept," she said, with a fist-bump. "Oh, don't forget you promised Abby Gatewood you'd see Jenna in pre-op holding before surgery."

"Believe me, that's one appointment I'm not going to miss. I have plenty of time. Her surgery's not until this afternoon. I'm sure the inquisition will be over by then."

"Are you sure? I thought it was this morning."

"No. It's on the schedule for one."

Shaking her head slowly, Roxanna said, "You better check, Dr. Flanigan. I looked at the schedule right before you got here. I'm positive Dr. Nichols has Jenna on the OR schedule for eight. Do you want me to call the OR to verify the time?"

"I'll do it."

Jacey walked across the room and picked up the phone and dialed the OR.

"Operating room, this is Kendra."

"Hi Kendra, it's Dr. Flanigan. Can you please tell me what time Jenna Gatewood's surgery is scheduled for?"

"She's the first case, Dr. Flanigan. In fact, she's in pre-op holding right now. We were a little delayed waiting for the on-call pump team to get here, but they're all here now, so they should be rolling back into the OR at any time."

"Did you say 'on-call team'?"

"Uh-huh."

Jacey felt her breath catch. "But—I thought Dr. Nichols had his own team, and never used the regular teams."

"That's true, but for some reason he decided at the last minute this morning to use one of our regular teams."

"Did he say why?"

"I—I don't know, Dr. Flanigan. That type of information is way above my paygrade. Would you like to speak to the charge nurse?"

"No, that's okay. Thanks for the information."

Confused by Nichols's sudden departure from his inviolate routine, Jacey slowly hung up the phone. Lost in thought, she started back toward the table she was using as the staging area for her presentation materials.

Suddenly, she stopped. "My God," she said.

Roxanna looked at her askance, betraying her confusion as to why her boss was visibly upset over a routine change in the operating room schedule.

"Are you okay, Dr. Flanigan? Your face is the color of chalk."

Panic-filled with the realization she only had a few minutes before Dr. Nichols would be laying a scalpel on Jenna's chest, Jacey sprinted toward the door.

"I'll meet you in the board room at eight thirty."

"Where are you going?"

"To the OR."

"Are you kidding?"

"Do I sound like I'm kidding, Roxanna? If you have to, stall for me."

"Don't lose track of the time," she warned. "I don't think being fashionably late would make the right impression. And I'm lousy at stalling. I'm sure Abby Gatewood will forgive you if you can't see Jenna before surgery."

"It's not *her* forgiveness I'm worried about—it's Jenna's."

FIFTY-EIGHT

"Go ahead and give her a kiss," the nurse anesthetist told Abby as she stood outside the entrance to the operating room. Abby leaned over the crib's siderail and gave Jenna a hug and then a soft kiss on her forehead.

"Don't be scared, baby," she whispered. "I'll see you real soon. I promise."

One of the nurses stepped forward and said, "I'll show you to the waiting room."

At the same moment, Jacey was sprinting across the bridge. When she reached the back stairwell, she flew down the two flights of stairs to the pre-op holding area and went straight to Jenna's cubicle, hoping she was still there. When she yanked back the curtain, her worst fear was realized. The room was empty.

"Shit," she muttered to herself. Praying she wasn't too late, she turned and raced down the corridor leading to the operating room entrance.

Stopping at the core desk, she asked, "Which OR is Jenna in?" The secretary was on the phone and held up a finger. After a few seconds, Jacey said, "Excuse me, but this is very important."

The woman covered the mouthpiece. Giving Jacey an annoyed look, she said, "I'm not sure what room your patient's in, but you're welcome to check the board. It's right behind you."

Jacey whirled around, her eyes leaping to the digital OR schedule. The first time she skimmed it, and she missed Jenna's name.

Forcing herself to calm down, she checked it again. This time she spotted it, and according to the board, she was already in her assigned operating room.

Jacey realized she couldn't go into the operating room in her street clothes, so she grabbed a plastic "bunny suit" and slipped it on over her clothes. With her next step, she was dashing down the corridor toward Jenna's operating room.

When she pushed open the doors to OR 4, she saw Jenna had already been moved from her crib to the operating table. The anesthesiologist was standing right behind her, holding an oxygen mask over her nose and mouth, just beginning to put her to sleep.

"I'm sorry, but this case has been canceled," Jacey announced with authority as she moved past the heart bypass machine. Her eyes were fixed on the anesthesiologist, who immediately removed the mask from Jenna's face and took a step back.

Meredith, the nurse in charge, approached. From the contemptuous look on her face, Jacey had no doubt she remembered her from the first time they'd met, when she'd unceremoniously tossed her out of Dr. Nichols's operating room.

"Excuse me, Dr. Flanigan, but the only person who can cancel this case is Dr. Nichols. I would assume you know that."

"I realize that's the usual protocol, but I just received information from the lab that mandates the case be canceled. I tried reaching Dr. Nichols a few minutes ago, but I wasn't able to."

"I suggest you take your concerns up with Dr. Nichols," she responded. "Until I hear otherwise from him, we're going ahead as scheduled. So, if you'll kindly step aside and allow us to do our job, we'd all very much appreciate it."

"I'll be happy to try contacting Dr. Nichols again, but for right now, I'm instructing you to take this patient back to pre-op holding."

With a poorly concealed smirk, Meredith stated, "I think we all understand that you have every reason not to be yourself this morning, Dr. Flanigan, but I don't care what your personal problems are or what you say. I'm not moving this patient until Dr. Nichols tells me to."

Jacey approached Meredith and spoke quietly. "I'm the only cardiologist in this room, which means my authority trumps yours. Now, I'm telling you for the last time to take Jenna back to the pre-op holding area. This is a patient safety issue that's way above your pay grade. If you refuse, I'll see to it you wind up in front of the Chief Nursing Officer." With a cold stare, Meredith crossed her arms in front of her. When she didn't move, Jacey added, "Don't test me, Meredith. I swear I'll call security and have you removed."

"I don't think that will be necessary," came a husky voice from behind her. "What's the problem?" Dr. Nichols asked.

"I'm sorry, sir," Jacey began. "But when I checked on Jenna early this morning to make sure she was ready for surgery, I thought her lungs sounded a little congested. I ordered a flu test. I just learned a few minutes ago that it's positive." Jacey felt Nichols's eyes on her. She'd never been a good liar, and by the way he was looking at her, she suspected now was no exception.

"That surprises me, because I checked her lab a half an hour ago. I didn't see a flu test had even been ordered." He walked over to one of the computers and signed on. "I realize you haven't been with us very long, Dr. Flanigan, but it's customary for the consulting cardiologist to call the surgeon directly if he or she has a pre-op concern."

"It was quite early, and since I assumed the test would come back negative, I saw no reason to disturb you. As I mentioned, I just called the lab a few minutes ago and got the results. They had just finished running the test, so it's not surprising the result hasn't been posted to the chart yet."

"But, just to be sure, you spoke to the lab personally, and they told you the flu test was positive."

"That's correct, and I'm assuming that under the circumstances, you wouldn't want to proceed with a general anesthetic and cardiopulmonary bypass for a patient who has the flu. It would be far too risky."

"Maybe it's nothing more than a laboratory error," Nichols suggested.

"That's of course a possibility, and the same thing crossed my mind."

"And?"

"I suggest we draw another blood sample. When we get the results, we can make a final decision about the timing of surgery. I understand it will delay things a little, but it's the only way to confirm Jenna doesn't have the flu."

Regarding her for a few moments with his arms pressed at his sides, Nichols finally said, "Our first priority is always the patient's safety. So, go ahead and order that second flu test. If it comes back negative, we can operate this afternoon. In the meantime, I'll go inform the parents of our change in plans."

"I'll call the lab right now," Meredith said.

Dr. Nichols straightened his surgical cap and then strolled toward the exit. As he passed Jacey, he said, "Actually, this may work out for the better. Now I can attend the Peer Oversight Committee meeting."

. . . .

As soon as Nichols was out of sight, Jacey walked out of the operating room knowing full well that her little ruse was, at best, a stopgap measure. Crossing her fingers, she prayed it would give her the time she needed.

In the heat of things, Jacey had forgotten Roxanna's advice and had lost track of the time. She cringed when she checked her watch. It was twenty after eight. Hurrying down the corridor, she couldn't help but wonder what difficult career decisions she could be facing before the day was through.

As she approached the elevators, she saw Abby staring out a large bay window that overlooked the hospital's small greenspace.

"I know what's going on," Jacey told her. "I know what they did to you and Tim."

"The only thing that matters anymore is Jenna, Dr. Flanigan. I hope you know what you're doing. By canceling her surgery, you may have put her life at risk. You have no idea who you're dealing with. If something happens to her, I'll never forgive you."

"Jenna was in grave danger. I'm asking you to trust me."

"I'm all out of trust, Dr. Flanigan," Abby said, as she turned and walked away.

FIFTY-NINE

Manhattan Children's Heart Hospital's executive board room was used primarily by the hospital's Board of Trustees for their monthly meetings. It was an ultra-modern chamber boasting plush theater-type seating for a hundred, integrated lighting, and a high-end video conferencing system.

In spite of her ordeal in the operating room, Jacey arrived at exactly eight thirty. While all of the committee members were already seated on the podium on one side of the large mahogany table, the last of the attendees were still finding their seats. The meeting was open to the entire medical staff, and owing to its unique circumstances, there wasn't an empty seat in the room.

Dr. Beyer met Jacey as soon as she came through the door and escorted her to the table on the podium and to one of the leather chairs that faced the committee members, with her back to the audience. Having avoided the unpleasant experience of having over a hundred pairs of judgmental eyes on her, Jacey was actually pleased she'd arrived at the last minute.

"You sure like to cut things close," he whispered with a wink, taking the seat next to her. Roxanna was seated on her other side and had already connected a laptop to the board room's video system in anticipation of Jacey's presentation. Jacey was rushing through some last-minute documents when the sound of Gault rapping his gavel on the wood sounding block raised her head.

Being the chairman, he sat in the center of the table, flanked by the other members of the committee.

"I'd like to call the meeting to order," he announced. "Dr. Flanigan, I assume you've reviewed the letter outlining why we've asked you to appear before the Peer Oversight Committee this morning."

"I have."

"To summarize briefly, a number of serious concerns have been raised regarding both your professional behavior and your competency to practice pediatric cardiology. The purpose of this meeting is to give you the opportunity to respond to a number of allegations. Afterward, the committee will deliberate and make any recommendations we may have to the Board of Trustees." Gault picked up a pen and slid a white legal pad closer to him. He raised his eyes to Jacey. "Do you have any questions before we begin?"

"Not at this time."

"Fine," he said, looking up and down the table at his colleagues. He reached forward, picked up a file and opened it. "The first agenda item concerns Bradley Sims, a three-year-old boy you saw in the post-op clinic, who recently underwent a VSD repair. Do you recall him?"

"I do."

"During that visit, were you informed by Mr. Sims that Bradley was scheduled for extensive dental work later this month?"

"Yes."

"A few days later, the father spoke to the dentist. He then called us, rather upset, to complain that you had failed to advise him about the absolute need for antibiotics before the dental work was done, and that you had failed to give him a prescription. We were obviously concerned, so we decided to review your note from Bradley's clinic visit." Gault leaned back in his chair and pushed his fingertips together. "Unfortunately, there was no note from you, which means you either ignored your responsibility to write one, or you simply forgot." Gault paused, and after regarding Jacey harshly for a few seconds, stated, "Before you answer, Dr. Flanigan, I would remind you that the writing of a clinic note after seeing a patient is a strict requirement of our medical-staff bylaws."

"I did write a note, and I definitely advised Mr. Sims of the unconditional need for antibiotics. I then wrote the prescription and handed it to him myself."

"Unfortunately, Dr. Flanigan, we have no way of verifying that."

"Other than taking the word of a colleague," Jacey said, raising a hand indicating her comment didn't call for a response. "Fortunately, I think I do have a way of verifying it."

"I'm sure we'd all be interested in learning how."

Jacey turned to Roxanna and gave her a nod. Roxanna stood up and approached the committee members with a stack of manila files in her hand. Making her way along the front of the table, she placed one in front of each of them. When she returned, she projected Bradley's medical chart on a large screen on a stand to the left of the committee.

Jacey made sure to face the committee as she spoke. "I direct your attention to the first document in your folder, which is an email from Dr. Chris Silva, one of the senior executives at Medicept. As most of you may already know, Medicept is MCHH's electronic medical record vendor. Dr. Silva states he was able to locate and restore my note to Bradley's chart. As you can see, the note includes my recommendation for antibiotics, and that Mr. Sims specifically requested I give him a handwritten prescription instead of an electronic one." Above the murmur in the room, she continued, "Dr. Silva also states categorically that my note was intentionally deleted from the chart."

"Excuse me, Dr. Flanigan, but what are you implying?" Dr. Milton Wabash, the Chief of Pathology, asked.

"I'm not implying anything. The committee asked me for an explanation. I'm providing one from a nationally recognized expert who confirms that I wrote a note and that somebody intentionally deleted it."

Gault held up a hand, halting any further explanation by Jacey, to allow the committee members to read Silva's report.

"Dr. Flanigan. I find it strange that our IT people didn't discover the same thing that Dr. Silva did," Gault said. Flipping back and forth between the pages, he asked, "Any idea why?"

"I can't speak intelligently to the expertise of our IT Department, Dr. Gault. I suggest you direct your concerns to them."

"Oh, you can rest assured I will."

Dr. Constance McCord, a highly respected and venerable pediatric cardiologist, raised her hand and was recognized by Gault.

"This report from Dr. Silva seems to provide definitive proof that Dr. Flanigan is telling the truth and that we've made a rather large error." She removed her reading glasses, leaned forward, and set her eyes on Gault. "It appears we owe Dr. Flanigan an apology."

"That might be a little premature."

"Then I suggest we move on to your next area of concern," McCord stated, in a disapproving tone.

"These concerns aren't mine, Dr. McCord; they're the committee's."

Dr. Nichols raised his hand. "I'd like to point out that locating your note doesn't change the fact that the patient's father insisted you didn't discuss the need for antibiotics with him. I'm afraid it's your word against his," he added, tossing the report down in front of him. "Are you really asking us to believe that Mr. Sims's memory is that bad? And what reason would he have for lying?"

"Since I was prohibited by our hospital attorney from speaking to him, I have no idea how sharp his memory is, or, for that matter, what motivated him to say what he did."

Red-faced, Gault stated, "Dr. Flanigan, I hope you're not implying that this committee would in any way act in a manner—"

Alexa Delacour said, "I tend to agree with Dr. McCord's suggestion that we move on."

With his lips pressed together, Gault tapped the conference table with the back of his pen for a few seconds before continuing. "Dr. Flannigan, we have a report that you were discovered in the Research Center in the middle of the night. The security guard reported you were pretending to be using a microscope." Looking up and with a disapproving shrug, he asked, "Would you care to comment?"

"It's true."

"Do you have an explanation?"

"Absolutely. I went to the Research Center to obtain a blood sample that had been drawn from Marc Saunderson during his code blue. When I informed you that I was concerned he'd been the victim of a medication error, you made it clear that you didn't agree and specifically instructed me to drop the matter."

"I remember our conversation. Your recollection regarding my response is accurate. Since you decided to ignore my request, perhaps you'd like to tell us why."

"That evening, I was able to get a sample of Marc's blood from the Research Center's laboratory and have it analyzed. If you'll take a look at the report in your folder, you'll see Marc Saunderson had sildenafil in his blood. Obviously, it was not a drug given to him intentionally during the code blue."

Another buzz filled the room, which prompted Gault to raise a hand to restore order.

"Sildenafil should never be given to a patient with Marc's diagnosis," Dr. McCord said. "To do so would be a tragic medication error that would likely lead to a cardiac arrest."

While Jacey watched Gault shake his head as he reviewed the laboratory report, Dr. Nichols spoke up. "You may be right about this patient accidently receiving a dose of some drug, but that still doesn't excuse your unauthorized entrance into the Research Center and seizure of the blood sample."

"I think it does," Dr. McCord was quick to point out.

"Excuse me, Dr. McCord, but my comment was directed at Dr. Flanigan."

"Excuse me, Dr. Nichols, but mine was directed at you. Please extend me the courtesy of allowing me to complete my thought," she told him. "Now, if I understand this correctly, a new physician in our department came to a senior heart surgeon with a significant concern regarding the safety of her patient, and for all intents and purposes, we told her to go jump in a lake. I think her perseverance reflects great professionalism and devotion to her patient. An objective observer would probably say we should be praising her instead of chastising her."

"I'm not sure we'd all agree with that," Nichols said.

"Perhaps this committee should be concerning itself with how such an inexcusable medication mistake could have occurred," Dr. Delacour stated. "I strongly recommend we initiate a root cause investigation immediately to get to the bottom of this serious error."

"Perhaps that question would be better addressed at our next Clinical Effectiveness Committee meeting," Nichols said. "For now, it's the responsibility of this committee to complete our agenda, which means an explanation from Dr. Flanigan as to why she violated a strict hospital policy that prohibits undertaking research projects and chart reviews without IRB Committee approval."

"I had major concerns about certain patient safety issues I'd observed. The only way to get to the truth was by reviewing the charts of the patients in question."

"Why didn't you go through normal channels?" Dr. Ben Morris, one of the emergency room physicians, asked.

"There was an urgency to my concerns. It normally takes at least six weeks for the IRB approval process. I didn't feel it was safe to wait," Jacey answered. "I believe the committee should know that the information I uncovered will go a long way in answering your questions about my fitness to practice medicine."

With purposeful eyes, she scanned the committee members. "If you'll allow me, I'd like to share those findings with you."

Jacey expected Gault to respond with a resounding no, but when she looked at him, she saw concern and uncertainty on his face. He covered his mouth with the palm of his hand and gazed across the audience.

Nichols came to his feet. "I strongly oppose that request. What Dr. Flanigan thinks she discovered is clearly outside the business of this committee. The point is, Dr. Flanigan, you violated a strict hospital policy. Your reasons for doing so are irrelevant." He turned to Gault. With a fisted hand, he tapped the table a few times. Jacey noted his complexion had reddened.

"I'm not sure all of us would agree with you," Dr. McCord said.

With a sweeping arm gesture, Nichols said, "I'd like to make a motion that the committee refuse to listen to Dr. Flanigan's findings."

"I'll be the first to oppose it," McCord was quick to announce.

Jacey looked again at Gault, who remained conspicuously silent. He tapped his lips with the fingertips of his steepled hands.

"Dr. Gault, I'd like a vote on my motion, sir," Nichols demanded.

After a few seconds, an anxious silence fell over the room and all eyes turned to Gault.

"A vote won't be necessary," he said. "I'm afraid there's been a mistake, for which I take full responsibility." Jacey immediately detected a loss of self-importance in his voice and manner.

"Excuse me?" Nichols said.

"I serve on the IRB Committee," Gault explained. "I'm afraid that I completely forgot until right now that Dr. Flanigan came to me and asked for preliminary approval to start her chart reviews. I told her to go ahead. I'm sure she didn't mention it this morning to save me the embarrassment my poor memory may have caused me."

Nichols said, "With all due respect, Adam, that's a bit hard to believe."

"Nevertheless, it's true. I apologize to the committee and to Dr. Flanigan. The blame lies entirely with me."

Jacey was stunned. Gault was lying, of course, but his unexpected display of fairness and willingness to consider he was wrong was the last thing she expected, irrespective of how persuasive she thought she might be in her own defense.

"There's still the matter of her insubordinate behavior—let's not forget about that," Nichols hurried to remind the committee members.

Gault said, "I think the business of this committee would be best served if we moved any further discussion of Dr. Flanigan's alleged unprofessional conduct to the end of the agenda. Right now, I believe it's more important we hear what she discovered from the research she did."

"That's totally inappropriate and out of order," Nichols stated.

"I'm sorry, Dr. Nichols, but I don't agree," Gault said.

"Nor do I," Dr. McCord said. "It appears Dr. Flanigan has compiled information that's crucial for our medical staff to hear. It's quite possible that what she's discovered may be of far more importance to this hospital than listening to more baseless accusations against her."

Nichols frantically waved a hand in front of him, and in a voice that soared, he said, "Adam, you don't have the authority, nor the—"

"Dr. Nichols, I remind you that as chairman of this committee, it's my prerogative to alter the agenda in any way I deem appropriate. If you have a problem with that, I'd suggest you take it up with the Chief of Staff and have me removed. In the meantime, we're going to hear what Dr. Flanigan has to say." Pushing his chair back, he added calmly, "I think now would be an excellent time for a fifteen-minute break."

SIXTY

Well before the fifteen minutes had expired, everybody in the room had retaken their seats. Leaning nervously forward in her chair, waiting for Gault to reconvene the meeting, Jacey pressed a calming hand to her brow. Then Gault began.

"Dr. Flanigan, I think the best way to handle this is for the committee to turn the floor over to you," Gault said. "However, we would like to reserve the right to ask you questions."

It was the moment she'd hoped and prepared so hard for. Jacey reminded herself to stay calm and focused. The meeting had gone well so far, but one misstep might be all that it would take to spell disaster for her.

"Thank you, Dr. Gault," she said. "The information I'm about to present is included in the second file that's being distributed to you now." Jacey paused to take a sip of ice water and clear her throat before continuing, "During the past eighteen months, one hundred and twenty children had an operation at MCHH to repair their VSD. I reviewed each of their charts and discovered something quite perplexing regarding their recoveries from the operation."

Jacey cast a look in Roxanna's direction, who gave her a short nod of encouragement. Jacey continued, "I found that these children fell into two very distinct groups: the first group's post-operative course with respect to complications and days in the hospital was routine and consistent with other children in the country undergoing the same operation. But the second group, which was composed of thirty-five patients, was dramatically different."

"In what way?" Gault asked.

"They recovered at a remarkable rate and suffered no surgical complications. In almost every case they went home the day after surgery, which is days sooner than other children here at MCHH and at other children's hospitals across the country."

"I'm not sure I understand the significance of what you're telling us, Jacey," Dr. Delacour stated. "It sounds like you're commending MCHH for attaining outstanding surgical results."

"I wish that were the case, but unfortunately, nothing could be further from the truth."

"Could you be more specific?" asked Dr. A. R. Woodruff.

"Yesterday, I performed an ultrasound on a one-year-old boy who'd undergone a VSD repair about a month ago. He was one of your patients, Dr. Nichols. Your operative note stated that you sewed in a synthetic patch to close the hole between the two ventricles of his heart. His name is Luke Winslow."

"I'm familiar with the patient. What's your point? I did an ultrasound the day he was discharged. It clearly showed the surgical outcome was perfect. I certainly hope you have something of more importance to share with us than one routine post-op ultrasound."

"The ultrasound I performed on Luke yesterday didn't show a patch. In fact, it showed a perfectly normal heart. There was no evidence he ever had a VSD."

Dr. Gault again raised his gavel to silence a sudden boisterous outbreak in the room.

"What in God's name are you talking about?" Nichols demanded, pounding his fist on the table. "I just told you. I personally did the ultrasound the day he was discharged, and it showed undeniably that a patch was in place. It's all documented in his medical record."

Jacey continued calmly, "You're correct. Your ultrasound report is in his chart, and I'm not disputing that it shows a patch." Jacey motioned to Roxanna. A moment later, the lights in the room dimmed. "The ultrasound images you're looking at are from the ultrasound I did on Luke yesterday. As you can plainly see, there's no patch visible. The next set of images are from the ultrasound Dr. Nichols performed the day he went home. On that ultrasound, there's definitely a patch present."

Nichols was quick to say, "I'm sure this—this discrepancy Dr. Flanigan is referring to is nothing more than some technical glitch with the ultrasound, or two patients getting mixed up. What's far more important, and what should be obvious to everybody on the committee, is that her career is in grave jeopardy and that she'd say or do anything to save herself."

"It appears we have a bit of a dilemma here," Dr. Delacour said. "Dr. Nichols is correct when he points out that one post-operative ultrasound really doesn't prove anything. It is quite possible that this peculiar finding is nothing more than some technical problem."

"I agree again," Jacey said. "And that's precisely why I arranged to do ultrasounds on seven other patients who had undergone a patch VSD repair within the last eighteen months. Now, all of these patients, just like Luke, had an ultrasound performed the day they went home after their operation, and every one of those studies showed a normal patch in place."

"Who authorized those visits?" Nichols demanded to know.

"I did," Jacey answered, while she projected new ultrasound images on the screen. "As you can see from the ultrasounds I did yesterday, the findings are identical to Luke's—there are no patches present in any of them. I would again remind the committee that each of these children underwent an ultrasound the day they were discharged that clearly showed a patch."

"My God," Dr. McCord said, slowly raising her hand to cover her mouth.

"With all due respect," Dr. Delacour said, above the clamor of the audience. "You may be an excellent young pediatric cardiologist, but you're not a trained radiologist."

"Which is precisely why I asked Dr. Rayburn of our Radiology Department to have a look at the ultrasounds."

"I see Dr. Rayburn is here," Gault said. "Would you mind sharing your findings with us?"

Bridgette Rayburn stood up from her seat in the first row, joined Jacey, and took control of the laptop.

"I still don't see what any of this proves," Nichols said, his cheeks red and puffed from anger. "Obviously, we have a problem in our Radiology Department."

"Unfortunately," Dr. Rayburn began, "I don't think that's the explanation. After Dr. Flanigan briefed me on her concerns, I studied the two ultrasounds from each child with extreme attention to detail. I believe I can say with certainty that in each case, the ultrasounds are not from the same patient."

"How's that possible?" Dr. Morris asked.

"I can only report the ultrasound findings, and I'm comfortable reporting to the committee that each of the ultrasounds done on the day the child was discharged were from a different patient than the one Dr. Flanigan did in clinic yesterday."

"That's absurd," Nichols yelled.

"I'm afraid the medical facts would argue differently, Dr. Nichols."

All at once, dozens of physicians waved their hands wildly in the air, seeking to be recognized. Dr. Rayburn stepped back, gave Jacey's hand a quick squeeze, and retook her seat.

"My God," Dr. McCord said.

After pounding his gavel several times on its sounding block, Gault finally was able to quiet the room.

"What are you suggesting?" Gault asked Jacey.

"The only conclusion I can reach is that a massive deception involving fraudulent medical records and x-rays has taken place at MCHH."

Dr. Carson Quillicy, the Chief of the Infectious Diseases Division, raised his hand and was recognized by Gault. He looked back and forth at the other committee members before speaking. "Please forgive the rantings of an old man, but I've remained silent long enough. I'm not sure what in perdition's going on around here, but I suggest we find out pretty damn quick, or we could find ourselves facing some pretty tough questions from more government agencies than we can shake a stick at."

"I'm not listening to any more of this preposterous fairytale," Nichols bellowed. "Nor will I sit here and be insulted by some wet-behind-the ears rookie." With his forehead beaded with perspiration, he stood up, descended the podium, and stormed out of the conference room.

"Excuse me for interrupting," came a voice from the second row. "But I'd like to have a word with Dr. Gault."

Leslie Santoro, MCHH's Chairman of the Board of Trustees for the past ten years, stood up. Assisted by a brass-embossed wooden cane, he made his way down the center aisle. An industrialist and noted philanthropist, Santoro was a no-nonsense man of conviction who rarely left anything unsaid. Jacey turned to face him. His eyes had already descended on hers. He slowly made his way onto the podium, stopping when he was directly in front of Gault. He nodded toward Gault's microphone, indicating Gault ought to cover it to keep their conversation from being conveyed to the entire room.

Leaning in over the conference table, he said in a quiet voice, "Adam, I think I'd be speaking for the entire hospital board when I suggest this meeting be adjourned immediately. We obviously have a catastrophic problem on our hands, and I hardly think this is either the forum, time, or place to address it."

"I agree."

"Offer any explanation you wish, but as of right now, this meeting's over. Once the room's cleared—and that includes the other committee members—I'd like to have a word with you and Dr. Flanigan."

With a flushed face, Gault slowly reached for his gavel.

Pushing his lips closer to his microphone, he announced, "I've decided it's in the best interests of the hospital if the committee tables the remainder of today's agenda." In spite of the outcries in the room, Gault took no questions, stating, "I'm sorry, but this meeting's adjourned."

With the objections still reverberating form every corner of the room, Gault stood up and made his way over to Jacey.

SIXTY-ONE

Jacey stayed seated while the room cleared, as did Gault. Santoro joined them at the table, sitting near Gault. Jacey could guess, but she couldn't know for sure where the conversation would take them. Realizing anything she'd say or disclose would be a tough bell to unring, she made sure to gather her thoughts.

Santoro was the first to speak.

"I guess there's no gentle way to put this, so I'll just say it: I'd very much like to hear the details of what you're—you're proposing occurred in this hospital."

"I can only speculate, sir."

He folded his arms in front of him, and with a furrowed brow, said, "Speculate away, Doctor."

Twenty minutes later, Jacey finished briefing Gault and Santoro on what she believed had occurred at Manhattan Children's Heart Hospital. She was surprised that neither of them halted her during her explanation to ask a question. Santoro was better at hiding his emotions behind a plain face than Gault was.

Santoro said, "I need a few hours to brief the other board members and to consult with our hospital attorneys regarding the best way to proceed. After we have a plan in mind, I'll call a meeting and brief the medical-staff leadership." He turned to Jacey. "I'm on unfamiliar ground, Dr. Flanigan. It's not often I find myself this conflicted. What you've uncovered could possibly sound the death knell for this hospital." He looked away and rubbed the back of his neck before turning toward her again. "But even if that comes to pass, it still pales in comparison to doing the right thing now. Irrespective of what you might think of us at the moment, as Chairman of the Board, I want to thank you."

Jacey was surprised when he said nothing further. She also got the feeling that he didn't expect her respond. She watched as he pushed himself to his feet and slowly made his way out of the conference room. Gault also stood up.

He spoke to her with his eyes turned toward the back of the room.

"I wouldn't know where to begin," he said in a voice painted with uneasiness. "But if you'll give me a little time, I'd like to sit down and talk with you."

"Of course," was all Jacey could manage.

He pressed his lips together in a tight line, nodded, and descended the podium.

Jacey stayed seated for a couple of moments before she gathered her things and strolled out of the room.

SIXTY-TWO

Santoro's office was only a few doors down from the executive conference room. He closed the door and sat down behind his mahogany desk. Adrift in thought, he stared for a time at an antique grandfather clock. After a time, he finally picked up the phone and placed a call to Dr. Delacour.

"I've been expecting your call," she said.

"Alexa, considering what has come to our attention, I don't see how we have any other choice but to immediately suspend all elective surgery until further notice."

"I completely agree. I've already contacted the OR Director and instructed her to cancel today's surgeries. As soon as we're off the phone, I'll call him back and advise him the moratorium will remain in effect until further notice."

"Obviously, if any of our patients need surgery on a more urgent basis, we'll arrange transfer to another hospital."

"Of course."

"We've known each other a long time, Alexa . . . and to be honest, I don't know if the hospital can survive this."

"We are and always have been a great institution. The price may be high, but I'm confident we'll figure out a way to get past this."

"I wish I shared your optimism. I'm going to call an emergency meeting of the board for this afternoon. I'll call afterward and update you."

"I'll look forward to speaking with you."

Santoro immediately made a second call, this time to Alice Corentin, the Chief Counsel for the hospital. She'd been present at the Peer Oversight Committee meeting, so there was no need to brief her. Their conversation was a short one. He placed the phone back on its cradle. His face harbored the look of a pummeled prize fighter, too breathless and too beaten to answer the bell for the final round.

Removing his wire-rim glasses, he slipped them into the breast pocket of his gray blazer. Slowly massaging the bridge of his nose, he never would have imagined a day would come when he'd have to instruct the hospital's Chief Counsel to call the FBI to report the suspicion of major illegal activity at MCHH.

In spite of everything else preying on his mind, Santoro kept coming back to the same question: what in God's name would compel a group of people to act in such a heinous and despicable fashion?

SIXTY-THREE

After the meeting, Jacey went straight to her office. She anticipated being set upon by her fellow physicians for more information, but to her surprise, her phone didn't ring once, and not a single knock was heard at her door. When she'd exited the conference center, she'd received a number of encouraging comments and a few thumbs-up from those who were still standing outside the room in small groups, but down to the last attendee, none of them pressed her for more.

She basically hid out for the rest of the day, busying herself with anything that might divert her thoughts from the Peer Review Committee meeting. Even though she'd prevailed and was certain she'd be completely exonerated of any and all allegations and wrongdoing, she wasn't overwhelmed with feelings of vindication. She called her father to inform him of the good news.

"Hi, Daddy."

"What happened?"

"The meeting ended a little while ago."

"And?"

"Everything went well. By tomorrow at this time, I'm pretty sure I'll receive an official letter from administration informing me that I'm a valued member of the medical staff and that my future at MCHH couldn't be rosier."

"That sounds to me like complete vindication. How come I'm not getting the feeling that you're doing a victory dance?"

"I guess the shock of things hasn't worn off yet."

"And I guess that's to be expected," he said. "

"I think I stirred up some pretty serious problems for the hospital."

"That they deserved."

"Well, I'm not denying that at least some of them did some pretty horrible things . . . but it's not like they haven't done a lot of great work in the past."

"It's not about the hospital. You did what you needed to do in the name of patient protection. What the future holds for the hospital is beyond your control," he said.

"I guess I have a few doubts."

"You stood by your principles. That's only hard to do when times are inconvenient. We talked about this the other night: your principles only mean something when it becomes difficult to stand by them."

"I guess so."

"I thought we'd talk about your future, but it sounds to me like you've had enough for one day . . . so, maybe that's a conversation for another time."

"Thanks, Daddy. I'll call you later."

Jacey thought about her call with her father. She couldn't imagine they'd believe such a letter would be enough to square things for the way she'd been treated. But it didn't really matter. It was Jacey's guess that Mr. Santoro and Dr. Gault would have much graver issues to consider in the weeks to come than her future.

At a few minutes past four, Jacey decided to call it a day. She hoped she'd be able to sneak out of the hospital without being ambushed by any of her colleagues anxious to hear more of the details of what she'd discovered. Her plan for the evening was equally banal. She'd order in dinner and then curl into the corner of her couch with a pint of chocolate chip ice cream and try to unload her mind by watching an old movie on television.

She was just about to shut down her computer when she was alerted to the arrival of a new email. It was from Alexa Delacour, requesting a meeting tomorrow morning at ten in Jacey's office. She was hardly surprised, expecting she'd be receiving many such requests over the next few days. Being that Dr. Delacour was the highest-ranking member of the Cardiac Surgery Division, it made sense she'd be the first one to knock at her door. Jacey leaned over her desk, accepted the meeting, and flipped the lid of her laptop down.

Before leaving the office, she reached for the phone and placed the call she'd been considering making since noon. When she was finished, she gathered her things together and headed out of her office. In spite of being beyond anxious to get home, she knew there was one stop she had to make before leaving the hospital.

SIXTY-FOUR

Making her way to the pre-op unit, Jacey crossed over the sky-bridge from the clinic building to the hospital. Once she arrived on the unit, she went straight to Jenna Gatewood's room. When she opened the door, she saw Abby sitting in a rocking chair with Jenna on her lap, reading her a story. The moment Abby's eyes fell on Jacey, she put the picture-book down.

"How are you doing?" Jacey asked.

"We're okay. I thought you might stop by today."

"I'm going to discharge Jenna. The hospital's not going to be doing any elective heart surgery for the next few weeks, which means there's no reason you can't take Jenna home right away."

"No elective surgery?" Abby asked. Jacey nodded. "From what I've heard, you had something to do with that."

Jacey wasn't naive to the fact that hospital gossip generally flies around like a whirlwind, but as a rule, that was amongst the staff, not the patients and their families.

"Let's just say the hospital has some problems to work out," Jacey said.

Abby stole a peek at Jenna, who had fallen asleep. Gently coming to her feet with Jenna cradled in her arms, she walked across the room, set Jenna down in her crib, and covered her with a blanket. After leaning down and kissing her cheek, Abby turned to Jenna.

"I suspect you're aware of what Tim and I have gone through for the past year and a half. I'm not going to make any excuses for our decisions. As long as Jenna stays safe, I'll find a way to live with everything else. I'm sure if Tim were standing here next to me, he'd agree." Jacey could see from the dire twist to her mouth, she was struggling to maintain her composure. "I'm a born worrier, and I just pray what happened today won't put Jenna at risk."

Jacey wanted to tell Abby that her nightmare was over and that she had nothing to worry about, that Jenna was safe and out of harm's way. She also wanted to tell her that Dr. Nichols's plan for Jenna was far more draconian than a simple skin incision on her chest. But Jacey also knew the best course at this point was to say nothing.

"As I said, I'm going to arrange for Jenna's discharge, but before you take her home, I'd like to do one final cardiac exam and officially document in her medical record that her heart is completely normal and always has been."

"Thank you, Dr. Flanigan. I appreciate that." Jacey removed her stethoscope from around her neck, walked over to the crib and began her exam.

"I know very little of what went on in this hospital this morning, but I'm praying it's the end of the most frightening dream any parent could ever imagine," Abby said to Jacey. "Tim was the most incredible father. I'm sorry he's not here to see what's happened. I can only hope his death in some way helped bring these people to justice."

"I have no way of saying anything for sure, but I'm confident this is the beginning of a new life for you and Jenna."

"I guess there's a part of me that's petrified they'll hold the parents equally responsible."

"I think a lot of people would feel you and Tim and the other parents were as much the victims as your children were."

With a forced smile, Abby crossed her fingers and held them up for Jacey to see.

"Should I make an appointment for Jenna to see you in the clinic?"

"If you and your beautiful daughter are ever in town, please come see me, but only to say hi—no medical appointment is necessary."

"I'd like that," Abby said, choking back her tears as she walked over and gave Jacey a huge hug.

SIXTY-FIVE

By seven p.m., Jacey had finished dinner and moved into the living room. She decided to pass on the ice cream in favor of a hot mug of French-vanilla coffee. She was reaching for her TV remote when the doorbell rang. She set the mug down on a glass-top coffee table and made her way to the front door. After a quick look through the peephole, she inhaled a settling breath and opened the door.

Both the man and woman standing in front of her held up their FBI badge wallets.

"Good evening, Dr. Flanigan. I'm Special Agent Elias Grady," the man said, lowering his wallet. He was tall with a bushy salt-and-pepper mustache. "This is Special Agent Maggie Kurdock."

"Thank you for coming. Please come in."

"We appreciate you calling the office," Kurdock said.

After hanging up their coats, Jacey escorted them into the living room and gestured toward the couch. She sat in a club chair directly across from them. She offered them something to drink, which they declined.

"Rumor at the hospital has it that you're going to be talking to a lot of people, starting tomorrow," Jacey said.

"We spent most of the afternoon with the hospital's attorneys and Mr. Santoro, trying to gather as much preliminary information as we could," Grady said. "Obviously, you're the key person we want to talk to. We're pleased you reached out to us before we contacted you."

"It wasn't too difficult a decision."

"From the limited information we have," Kurdock said, "you've uncovered some extremely disturbing activities at MCHH. We're anticipating a comprehensive and far-reaching investigation."

"I think you'll discover that what occurred at MCHH is undisputable," Jacey assured Maggie.

"We'll be dealing with a parent corporation that's valued well into the millions. When you have access to the type of legal firepower they do, nothing's indisputable. Believe me, whether they've had a hand in this conspiracy or not, protecting their reputation and image will be in the front of their minds," replied Grady.

"If you don't mind me asking," Kurdock began, "are you getting much pressure from the hospital on what to share with the authorities and the media?" Her Scottish accent was anything but subtle, leaving Jacey wondering what path she'd taken that had led her to becoming a special agent in the FBI.

"Nobody at the executive or medical-staff leadership level has pressured me. I assume, for the most part, they're highly principled people who wouldn't expect me to compromise my own principles. Tomorrow morning I'm scheduled to meet with Dr. Alexa Delacour. She's the Chief of Cardiac Surgery. The meeting's part of the reason I called you."

"As Special Agent Kurdock mentioned, we're grateful you reached out to us. We could ask you questions all night, but perhaps it would be better to begin with you telling us why you asked for this meeting."

Jacey didn't respond to his request at first. Her mind drifted briefly, making her almost oblivious to the fact that there were two FBI agents sitting across from her. She didn't notice when Kurdock and Grady exchanged a puzzled look.

"Dr. Flanigan?" Kurdock asked. "Was there something specific you wanted to discuss with us?" Jacey instantly regained her focus and moved forward in her chair. A look of resolve spread across her face.

"Yes, there most certainly is," she told them.

216

SIXTY-SIX

After a restless night's sleep, Jacey was out of bed at sunup. She didn't waste any time getting to the hospital and finishing her morning rounds. By nine-thirty, she was back at her desk, catching up on her medical records. She'd only been working about fifteen minutes when she heard three quick knocks at the door.

She closed the lid of her laptop and said, "Come in."

"Good morning," Alexa said. "I know I'm a little early. I hope you don't mind."

"Of course not. Have a seat."

"Thanks for finding time to meet with me on such short notice. As you can imagine, things are a little crazy around here. I'm almost afraid to ask how the rest of your day went yesterday."

"It wasn't too bad. I kind of kept my head down."

"That was probably a smart move. Before we get started, tell me—how are you doing?"

"Under the circumstances, I'd say I'm okay."

"Good," she said, settling into the chair across the desk from Jacey. "Now, as Chief of Surgery, I think it's critically important that you and I chat about the issues you've brought to our attention. And after we do that, what's the best way to handle things, moving forward."

Alexa moved back in her chair and crossed her legs at her ankles. "I know you haven't been with us very long, so it's understandable that you don't have the same . . . same emotional ties to MCHH that some of us veterans do. But I think we should all try and get on the same page when it comes to dealing with the investigation into the allegations you made."

"Allegations?"

Alexa held up both hands as if she were halting traffic. "It's just a term. I understand how you feel, but for now, both the hospital administration and corporate feel that's what we should call them."

"I see."

"Don't misunderstand me. The Board of Trustees and the physician leadership expect that we'll all fully cooperate with the FBI investigation, but at the same time, do everything we can to protect the good name of the hospital."

"Doing those two things at the same time might turn out to be a neat trick."

"I think you're reading too much into this. I think the board is simply asking that we be very careful about what we say until we have all of the facts."

Jacey leaned forward, interlaced her fingers, and set her hands on her desk. "Maybe instead of trying to figure out some way out of this mess, those responsible should just own up to what they did."

"Which means what, exactly?"

"Take responsibility for being criminals who intentionally used unconscionable medical practices against innocent infants and children."

Grim-faced, Alexa drummed the arm of her chair. When she was finished, she pressed her lips together and stood up.

"It appears you've already made up your mind about this problem, so I don't see much reason to continue this conversation. Since I didn't conduct a huge investigation as you did, I'm not in a position to tell you what to do. I guess I was too busy taking care of patients to play private eye." She turned and started toward the door. "And I guess I'm not as positive as you are that anything criminal went on in the hospital."

"I think you're quite positive."

With a puzzled expression, Alexa inquired, "Do you actually think I was involved in any of this?"

With a hard stare, Jacey answered, "Up to your eyeballs."

SIXTY-SEVEN

Alexa stood at the door for a few seconds, but then, instead of walking out of the office, she returned to her seat.

"Just what do you think you know, Jacey?"

"The same things you do."

"Excuse me?"

"I think we're both aware that a substantial number of children were carefully selected. Over the following few years, each of them had a false medical history created that claimed they had a serious heart defect. At a predetermined time, they were referred to MCHH, where they were admitted and then underwent a sham operation—an operation this hospital claimed repaired a VSD they never had."

"Phony medical records and a make-believe operation? That sounds more like a bedtime story than a rational explanation for a few irregularities."

Jacey stood up and leaned over her desk. She could feel her blood beginning to boil.

"I don't believe any of these children were ever placed on cardiopulmonary bypass or had their hearts touched by a surgical instrument. Once a skin incision was made, no further surgery took place. A couple of hours later, the incision was closed and the child was sent to the recovery room, just as if they'd really had a VSD repair."

"That's quite an accusation. You realize that what you're suggesting would mean everybody in the operating room would have to have been complicit in this highly calculated scheme of yours."

"I'm not suggesting it. I'm stating it as a fact."

"And the parents? I assume your conspiracy theory includes that they were all enthusiastically agreeable to this crime as well."

Jacey sat again, but continued in a steely voice, "Fifteen of the thirty-five patients were adopted. I imagine a young couple unable to have a child by any other means or in dire financial straits might be desperate enough to make a deal with the devil, especially when they were assured that once the operation was over, their child would lead a perfectly normal life, never again to be contacted by anybody connected to MCHH."

"That's a little light on details and logic, to say the least."

"I'm sure once the FBI has completed their investigation, everything will be abundantly clear."

"You seem so sure of yourself, but I think the facts may tell a different story," Alexa said, still speaking with a plain face in a calm tone of voice.

"The facts? There's only one fact that matters—and that is that trusted members of this hospital willfully participated in a despicable crime against children and were also involved in several homicides."

"Are you finished?"

"Actually, I'm just getting started," Jacey said.

"I'm not saying all of this doesn't make for good theater, but I came here hoping to talk with you about protecting the good name of our hospital."

"If you're here trying to enlist me to help in damage control . . . well, you better order in lunch, because you're going to be sitting there awhile. Just tell me I'm wrong."

"Why? Would it do any good?" Alexa asked, with a blasé giggle. "You know, Jacey, sooner or later you're going to have to make an important decision: either you'll continue to keep your head buried in the sand about the future of children's heart surgery, or you'll have the courage to share in the responsibility of fighting for the highest possible standards."

"Nice speech, but if it means having a hand in some depraved criminal scheme . . . well, it would be the easiest decision of my life."

"You simply don't understand. You have no idea what direction unenlightened people who have no daring could take children's heart surgery in the next ten years. The results could be catastrophic."

"Are you trying to rationalize away the evil acts of a group of misguided individuals? Is that what you're trying to sell me?"

"I'm not trying to sell you anything."

"Then what are you doing?"

"I'm trying to educate you." After a shallow sigh, Alexa asked, "Do you know how many children's hospitals there are within a hundred miles of here that have a cardiac surgery program?"

"Twenty-three," Jacey answered with no hesitation.

"That's exactly right. Now, there's only a finite number of children who need heart surgery every year, which means MCHH and these other hospitals are always fiercely competing for these patients. As I'm sure you know, when too many hospitals are vying for a limited number of patients, the surgical experience gets diluted, and quality of care suffers. Complications and death rates soar. The exact opposite occurs when only a few hospitals provide all the surgery—their experience level goes up, which translates to far better surgical outcomes."

"I think we're all pretty much aware of that."

"As is the government and every insurance company that's paying for these operations and hospitalizations. They're also painfully aware that too many hospitals doing a limited number of cases sends their costs skyrocketing. Many of them think the answer is instead of having twenty hospitals or more doing specialized surgery, designate the best two or three and send all the children who need heart surgery to one of them."

"Centers of Excellence."

"Exactly."

"Which I suspect is the reason behind all of this treacherous behavior," Jacey said.

"We have to do whatever's necessary to make sure MCHH is named a Center of Excellence. And how do you think that decision is going to be made?" Alexa leaned forward and continued, "Let's use pediatric heart surgery as an example. When Centers of Excellence become a reality, how do you think the government and insurance companies will decide which two or three hospitals out of twenty-three they'll designate as the centers?"

"I imagine they'll use several means, but the most important will be the STS National Heart Surgery Databank."

"I agree. It's really the only objective and accurate way we have of comparing one hospital's surgical performance to another," Alexa said. "And you don't have to be a Rhodes Scholar to realize the hospitals that are the highest ranking in the databank will be the ones selected as Centers of Excellence."

"And the best way to do that would be performing just as many sham operations as necessary, having perfect results, and fraudulently submitting them to the databank."

"The enlightened, forward-thinking leaders in health care hear the death knell ringing for the old ways."

"And I assume you count yourself amongst them."

Alexa grinned as if somebody was trying to sell her a parcel of swamp land. "I'm not confessing to anything, Jacey. But I am saying there is a very influential group of MCHH physicians and top-level executives at corporate who believe Centers of Excellence will play a critical role in MCHH's future. And they're always looking for dynamic people who are like-minded.

"By submitting a certain number of MCHH patients with perfect outcomes to the national databank, we guarantee our ratings will be amongst the highest in the country, which is exactly the position we want to be in." She grinned, shrugged her shoulders a bit, and added, "Why should we compete on a level playing field?"

"Even if there were major changes in health care delivery and a system of Centers of Excellence was adopted, MCHH would likely be selected as one of them legitimately, being based purely on merit."

"Maybe, but why should we gamble the survival of this hospital on something that's not a sure thing? Santoro and the rest of the Board of Trustees are endangering the very existence of MCHH. Their horse-and-buggy thinking will put us into a tailspin that we'll never be able to recover from. We're not a publicly funded, full-service children's hospital that can afford to lose a service or two and still remain financially viable. We provide one and only one service, and that's pediatric heart surgery. If we're not doing it, we're out of business. Our parent corporation considers MCHH to be their flagship hospital, specifically designated to promote the concept of exclusive, high-end, specialized hospitals. Centers of Excellence are critical to that strategy. It's the only model that will predictably eliminate competition and guarantee financial success for years to come."

"A couple of minutes ago, you said this is about delivering excellence in pediatric heart surgery. Now you're talking about financial windfalls," Jacey said. "Which one is it—money, or taking the best care of kids we're capable of?"

"Where is it written the two are mutually exclusive?" Alexa asked.

"I guess if all this came to pass, it wouldn't do you any harm."

"Hypothetically speaking, my position in the hospital and corporation would continue to skyrocket, MCHH would solidify its position as the most outstanding children's hospital in the country for heart surgery, and I'd make a pile of money."

"Hypothetically speaking," Jacey repeated cynically, to which Alexa responded with a smug grin. "You know, everything you claim will come to pass is nothing more than theories, what-if projections, and wishful thinking."

"I'm not sure I agree," Delacour said, shifting forward in her chair. "Assuming we continue our outstanding performance as documented by the national databank, there will be an announcement next year from the governor's office that Manhattan Children's Heart Hospital has been selected as the first Center of Excellence for pediatric heart surgery in the state. The designation will mark the beginning of a pilot program to test the concept."

"I hope that's one pilot program that never sees the light of day."

"I don't think they'll ask your opinion on the matter," Alexa assured her. "Listen, Jacey. I have no illusions. What we're trying to do is isn't for the faint of heart. As you get older, you'll realize people who make groundbreaking achievements oftentimes have to speak for those individuals who are less courageous."

"Like Jonathan Bice and Mitch Laraby? Who speaks for them?"

"They were both excellent doctors whose deaths were heartbreaking. But in the long run, their passing will save lives."

"Is that what we should tell Marc Saunderson's mother and the parents of the twenty-four other children who were either denied appropriate surgical care or whisked off to other, less-capable hospitals?"

"Patients like Marc who are profoundly ill and need urgent surgery are at high risk of dying," Alexa responded. "That's not something a hospital trying to keep their post-operative survival statistics with the national databank unblemished can allow. The smarter move is to either transfer those children to another hospital, or make sure they never see the inside of our operating room."

"Unblemished death rates? Just how evil can you be?"

"That's hardly the issue . . . anyway, as I suspected, trying to educate you is a lost cause."

"If you thought you'd be able to convince me that illegal and morally corrupt medical practices and murder are justifiable to ensure capturing a larger share of the heart surgery market, you're tragically mistaken."

Alexa stood up. "I hope you'll at least think about what we've talked about."

"I think that's one promise I can definitely make," Jacey told her. "Do you happen to remember a patient by the name of Charlie Struthers?"

"Not off the top of my head."

"Last July 12, Dr. Corbett scheduled him for a VSD repair. An hour into the case, the doctor developed a severe migraine. He informed the nurse that he wasn't sure if he could continue, and he asked her to call you to step in for him. You came to the OR but were only there for about ten minutes, because Dr. Corbett began feeling better. It's all in the nursing notes."

"Sounds like the type of thing that happens from time to time. Why are you telling me all this?"

"I found out Charlie's had some interesting health issues since the surgery. It's not important."

"I'm sure it's not, but if you're concerned, maybe you should take that up with Dr. Corbett. You're reaching, Jacey, and we both know it."

"Maybe. I guess that will be up to the FBI to decide. How they handle this whole thing is none of my business."

Alexa opened the door, but before stepping out into the corridor, she glanced back over her shoulder at Jacey.

"That's funny coming from you. I assumed you felt everything was your business."

SIXTY-EIGHT

Ten minutes after Alexa left her office, Jacey was still sitting at her desk, reliving every word of their conversation. Enraged at Alexa's coldhearted arrogance and cruelty, Jacey was slowly rotating her manager's chair when she heard a knock at her door.

"Come in."

Special Agent Maggie Kurdock walked in with a gratified smile.

"The equipment worked perfectly," she said. "We got it all—audio and video."

Jacey came out from behind her desk and met Maggie in the middle of the room.

"She was more talkative than I expected," Jacey said.

"I think when she realized you knew a lot more than she thought, she tried to do everything she could to get you to see the light and join their camp. I don't believe she felt she was at risk, because she didn't know she was being recorded. Talking with you one-on-one is nothing more than hearsay, from a legal standpoint."

"We were hoping for a confession. I'd hardly call it that."

"It may not have been a slam-dunk admission of guilt, but it was in the neighborhood. We'll let the Attorney General sort that out, but something tells me she doesn't have a prayer of saving herself."

"I hope not."

"You know, if you hadn't called us to request a meeting, none of this would have been possible."

"Dr. Delacour's pretty smart. It's possible she could figure this whole thing out and not take the bait."

"Maybe. The only good thing is it shouldn't take us very long to find out. It's a miracle that none of the children they operated on weren't seriously injured."

"Unless intent counts for anything," Jacey said.

"What do you mean?"

"Jenna Gatewood."

"Her surgery was canceled."

"The morning of her surgery, Nichols arranged for one of the regular pump teams to be in his room instead of his normal private team, which means he fully intended to completely open Jenna's chest and put her on the bypass machine. I think he planned to have her suffer some major complication before he started to actually operate on her heart."

"For what purpose?" Maggie asked.

"I think he figured he was playing it safe. He probably wanted be able to point to at least one patient who suffered a serious complication or worse to prove not every child he operated on with a VSD had a perfect result."

"Do you think Delacour knew?"

"I doubt it," Jacey answered. "I'm betting she's a lot smarter than he is and would've made him cancel Jenna's surgery if she'd known."

"Whatever the details, thank God they never operated on Jenna," Maggie said. "Our technicians are on their way over now to remove all of the surveillance equipment."

"In that case, I'll clear out and give them some space," Jacey said.

Maggie extended her hand. Jacey smiled and shook it.

"If you've got a little time to spare, this FBI Special Agent would like to buy you a cup of coffee."

"It would be my great pleasure," Jacey said, reaching for her purse.

As they started toward the door, Maggie said, "You know, I don't think you're giving yourself enough credit."

"I'm not sure I understand what you mean."

"Making that first call to us took an amazing amount of courage. It can't be easy turning in a fellow professional. You didn't have to do that. You had a choice."

"The funny thing is—I really didn't."

SIXTY-NINE

TWO DAYS LATER

After another sleepless night, Laine Saunderson pounded her pillow and then sat up in bed. Struggling to clear her grief-cluttered mind, she threw back the blanket, climbed out of bed, and quietly walked from the parent's suite into Marc's room.

For the past two days, she hadn't left his side for more than a few minutes at a time. The room was warm and filled with a lingering scent of illness. To her dismay, he still hadn't uttered a single word or responded to her in any way. The only encouraging thing was the doctors had been able to remove him from the ventilator, allowing him to breathe on his own.

Laine walked out of the room and then slowly down a long corridor until she reached the parent's lounge, where she poured herself a cup of coffee. She sat in one of the soft club chairs and sipped the fresh brew for a few minutes before returning to Marc's room. Strolling over to the window, she noticed a light glaze of dew had formed on the outside of the glass.

After a time, she returned to Marc's bedside. She reached down and curled her hand around his. When she felt tears about to rain down, she fought back by reminding herself to hold onto hope, and that according to the doctors, he still had a chance of regaining consciousness.

She leaned down and touched his pasty white lips. "I love you, Shrimp."

She stayed with him until ten, when she decided a walk might help lift her spirits. She went back into her room, put on some warm clothes, and then returned to Marc's bedside and kissed his forehead. Usually it was speckled with perspiration, but for the first time in days, it was dry. When she reached the door, she stopped, looked back, and said the same silent prayer she did every time she left the room.

. . . .

It was an hour later when Laine returned from her walk in Central Park. She was making her way over to the bedside when his nurse, Rebecca, entered the room, holding a Styrofoam container.

Handing it to Laine with an encouraging smile, she said, "I saw you coming down the hall. I thought you might like some coffee."

"Thanks."

As Laine brought the container to her lips, she looked down at Marc. At first, she was perplexed, but a few seconds later, her eyes widened in disbelief and her stomach fluttered.

"Did you put his giraffe under his arm like that?" she asked. "When I left, it was next to his leg."

Rebecca shook her head slowly. "I didn't touch it."

Laine's hand began to tremble. She lost her grip on the container. When it struck the ground, the lid flipped off, sending the coffee splashing in every direction across the floor.

"Don't worry about it," Rebecca said, heading to the door. "We'll have it cleaned up in no time."

"No, don't leave," Laine pleaded.

With her heart hammering, Laine inched her way closer to the bed. With each step, she prayed her eyes weren't deceiving her. Curled under Marc's arm was the giraffe his grandmother had made for him when he was a baby. As soon as he was able, he slept with it under his arm and wedged against his cheek. Still in disbelief of what might be happening, Laine saw the distressed look on his face had vanished. Reaching down, she touched his lips and mouth. His jaw muscles were relaxed, and he wasn't clenching his teeth.

"Everything's different," she uttered between choked breaths. "His breathing, his expression, his color . . . everything." Laine paused for a few seconds, realizing her cracking voice must have made it almost impossible for Rebecca to understand her. A nervous laugh escaped her lips.

"I'll call Dr. Flanigan."

Laine quickly reached behind her, pulled up a chair, and sat down. She inched her lips close to Marc's ear.

With her eyes awash with tears, she whispered, "Hey, Shrimp. It's Mommy. I'm right here. It sure looks like you're feeling better." He didn't respond, but Laine had no intention of giving up. "I've been so worried about you."

"Mommy, I'm sleepy."

Laine's hand covered her mouth as she looked away, sweeping away the tears that cascaded down her cheeks.

The door flew open, and Jacey and Joanna hurried to the bedside. Hovering over Marc, Jacey removed her stethoscope from around her neck. Laine stood up and took a few steps back. After a couple of moments, Jacey removed her scope and slowly turned and faced Laine. As she took a few steps closer, a larger-than-life smile spread across her face.

With her eyes heavy with tears, Laine hugged her and whispered, "I never thought I'd feel this type of sheer bliss again."

SEVENTY

The moment Special Agent Maggie Kurdock returned to the lobby after taking a phone call, she saw Grady standing next to the elevator, motioning her to hurry up. It was eleven forty-five p.m.

Grady tapped the button to summon the elevator. "They're upstairs in one of the empty unassigned physician offices. The Cyber Division guys were alerted the moment Dr. Delacour and her little helper signed on. I just got a call from the agent in charge. She told me Delacour just signed off. C'mon, let's get up there."

The elevator doors rolled open and they rode the elevator up to the fourth floor. Grady pointed the way, and they followed a wide corridor to the office where Delacour had signed onto the hospital computer system. Grady opened the door. Alexa Delacour was standing behind a shaggy-haired man seated at a desk with his head to the side of the monitor.

"Good evening, Dr. Delacour," Maggie said. Alexa slowly reached past the man and shut off the monitor.

"I'm Special Agent Kurdock and this Special Agent Grady. Do you mind telling us what you're doing in an unassigned doctor's office at midnight?"

"Excuse me, Special Agent. I've already met with two of your colleagues and fully answered all of their questions. What I'm doing right now is hospital and patient-care related. It falls under patient privacy laws, and I'm therefore not at liberty to discuss it with you. If you'd like to speak to me tomorrow about other matters, please call my office and make an appointment."

"We're sorry for the inconvenience, Doctor, but we do have to speak with you right now." Delacour exhaled a full breath, dropped her arms to her side, and gave them both a hard stare. She said nothing. Maggie took a couple of steps forward. "Dr. Delacour. We're here on official business. We can either talk here or we'll escort you out of this hospital and to our office, where we'll be happy to conduct this conversation. The choice is entirely yours."

"I guess you're not leaving me much choice, but I will be making a formal complaint about this."

"That's of course your right and up to you. Now, would you mind telling us what you're doing in an unoccupied office in the middle of the night?"

"I don't know why that should interest you, but if you must know, I was having some technical problems with my medical records."

"And the gentleman with you?" Grady asked.

"I'm not very techy. He works here in the hospital on our IT team. I requested his assistance, and he was kind enough to agree."

"I assume the problem you were having is now fixed," Grady said.

"As a matter of fact, it is."

"Why were you looking at video surveillance from the operating room?" Maggie inquired.

"Part of my job as Chief of Surgery is to investigate ways to improve the flow in our operating rooms."

"I see," Maggie said. "Is it also part of your job to delete segments from those videos?"

"I beg your pardon?"

"You deleted a segment from one of those tapes that showed your presence in the operating room during a surgery last July. It was a VSD repair done on Charles Struthers."

"I'm not sure your information is accurate, but if I did, it was an accident. As I said, I've been having computer issues."

"When we interviewed you, Dr. Delacour, you made it clear you had no knowledge of any irregularities of any type that might have occurred in the operating room over the last year or so."

"I'm aware of what I said."

"Charlie Struthers was one of the patients who underwent an orchestrated operation he didn't need."

"I'm sure you meant to say allegedly, Special Agent."

"The point is, one would assume the Chief of Surgery, standing three feet from a child undergoing a heart operation, would know if the child was on the bypass machine with his breastbone split down the middle having a large hole sewn up. Would you agree?"

"I guess it would depend on the surgeon," she answered with a shrug, "Other than that, I have no opinion on the matter."

"You didn't report anything out of the ordinary to the charge nurse," Maggie continued. "Nor did you file an incident report with the hospital administration. We also checked the minutes from the meetings of the Quality Assurance Committee, which you're the chair of, and you didn't report it there either." Maggie pulled up a chair, placed it right in front of Delacour, and sat down. "Do you see what I'm getting at here, Doctor?"

"Actually, I don't."

"I can only think of one reason why you'd delete the portion of Charlie Struthers's surgical video that clearly showed you were at the table assisting with the operation."

"Special Agent Kurdock. I've done my best to be open and cooperative with the FBI's investigation. But I'm not going to sit still while you sling wild accusations at me." Alexa stood up, and with an intense focus to her voice, added, "If you're too obtuse to understand what I'm saying, I'll spell it out for you: I'm not answering any further questions without my lawyer being present."

"That's your right," Grady said, as he stood up, walked over to the door, and opened it. The moment he did, two agents walked in. It took them a couple of minutes to read Delacour her rights and place her in handcuffs.

As she was being escorted to the door, she looked back and said, "I suspect you'll discover Dr. Flanigan's not the brilliant young doctor you think she is. She probably thinks she got all of us."

"I'm certain Dr. Flanigan is intelligent enough to know you got yourselves."

Grady and Kurdock both turned and faced the man from IT at the same moment.

"What's your name, sir?"

"David Barro."

"Have a seat, Mr. Barro," Grady told him. "We have a few questions we'd like to ask you."

As Barro cautiously moved forward, he said in a shaky voice, "I just work here. I was given a bunch of assignments, which I took care of. I didn't ask any questions, I just did what I was told, so I wouldn't lose my job."

"We totally understand, David," Maggie said. "But we'd still like to hear about all of those assignments you took care of."

David sat down in the chair. His chin slumped to his chest and his fingers began to tremble.

SEVENTY-ONE

It had been three days since Marc had emerged from his coma. Each time Jacey saw him, she was more overjoyed with the progress he was making. The evidence was convincing that he hadn't suffered any permanent brain damage from his code blue. At Jacey's recommendation to Laine, Dr. Gault took over his case. His condition was stable and, although he still was facing a major heart operation, Jacey was confident he'd come through it fine.

Walking off the unit, she followed a lengthy hallway leading her to the heart transplant unit. She'd been formally advised the Peer Oversight Committee had completely exonerated her of any wrongdoing. She was pleased of course, but the news did little to diminish the dismay that continued to plague her when she thought about all the infants and children who'd been victimized at MCHH. Whether the hospital would survive the devastating publicity and criminal indictments was anybody's guess. If they did, at best it would be a long road back.

She had almost arrived at the transplant unit when she spotted Dr. Beyer slowly heading toward her. His face was drawn, his shoulders slouched forward, and it was evident he hadn't given much thought to his appearance.

"Good morning," he said. "I suppose you've heard by now."

"I did, and if it means anything to you, everybody feels you did the right thing."

"I didn't even call a lawyer. A few hours after the committee meeting, I set up a meeting with the FBI, went down to their office, and offered to fully cooperate with the investigation."

"Did you make a deal?" she asked, noticing his pasty complexion and that the soft tissues that framed his eyes were puffed heavily with edema fluid.

"I didn't ask for a deal, Jacey. I simply confessed. I realized it was the only chance I'd have to redeem myself. Afterward, I went straight to see Leslie Santoro and resigned my position, effective immediately." Jacey didn't know what to say. She viewed him as a pathetic character but felt no sympathy for him.

"Now what?" she asked.

"I was just on my way to my office to finish packing up the last of my things. I don't know when they'll formally arrest me. It didn't enter into my decision to turn myself in, but I suspected you had a pretty good idea that I had gotten myself involved in something that was pretty unholy." He finally shifted his gaze in her direction. "Did you know?"

Jacey wasn't sure how to respond. She felt no obligation to disclose anything to him, but that changed when he'd asked her directly if she knew he'd been involved in the conspiracy. Not entirely sure she was doing the right thing, she decided not to sidestep his question.

"You were the only cardiologist to see the thirty-five children with VSD repairs in question in the clinic for their post-op visits," she explained. "Since we have nine pediatric cardiologists on staff, it seemed too odd to write off to coincidence. The other inexplicable thing was that you only saw those children once in the clinic. You then informed the parents their son or daughter never needed to return. That's hardly consistent with the long-term follow-up care that's an integral part of open-heart surgery in children. And, I thought it was strange that none of the parents questioned your recommendation that long-term follow-up care wasn't necessary." Jacey pressed her lips together for a moment and then added, "It wasn't very hard to connect the dots."

"But you didn't say anything to the FBI."

"I won't lie. I was conflicted by the choice, but you acted so quickly that . . . well, the problem kind of took care of itself."

"I see."

"I answered your question; I have one I'd like to ask you." He raised his eyes to hers and nodded. "How could you allow yourself to become involved in such a cruel crime against children? Was it about money?"

An uneasy grin materialized on his face. "Different things motivate different people, Jacey," he answered, removing his glasses and slipping them into his top pocket. "I don't care a whit about money; I never have. My whole professional life has been about this great hospital's Research Center. It's been our shining star since the day we cut the ribbon. Thousands of children and adults all over the world are alive today because of the countless breakthrough medical advances discovered in our Research Center."

He looked away briefly and then continued in a splintered voice, "I don't know anything about hardcore health care economics or the business of medicine. I somehow convinced myself that this hospital and its Research Center had to survive, irrespective of the cost. I was misguided—I acted like an old fool who'd lost his moral compass."

"Did you have any idea from the beginning to what extremes these people were prepared to go to?"

"No. Never. I swear. They told me no child would be harmed in any way."

"But when you learned that wasn't the case, you decided to say and do nothing. All you did was look the other way."

"I have no excuse, Jacey. All I can say is that I never knew it would come to this."

In a calm voice, Jacey answered, "Dr. Beyer, it came to this the first time you stood silently by and allowed a child to undergo an illegal operation that put their life at risk."

Without uttering another syllable or waiting for his response, Jacey turned her back on Nathan Beyer and walked away.

SEVENTY-TWO

Attorney Miles Cunningham followed the events at MCHH to the point of obsession. Having been complicit in the criminal conspiracy by arranging for the illegal adoption of more than twenty babies, Cunningham had no illusions about whether the FBI would soon be bearing down on him. He was painfully aware that there was no legal argument he could make that had any hope of saving him from many years in prison—or worse. As rapidly as he was able, he made the necessary arrangements to leave the country, with the intent of never being seen or heard from again.

Cunningham was seated in a tan leather club chair in the Sky Club Lounge in the Cincinnati International Airport, sipping on a sparkling water. Anxious to board his flight, he again checked the flight information board to make sure there wasn't a last-minute delay. Just as he did, one of the service associates approached.

"Excuse me, Mr. Cunningham. Your flight to Rome is ready for boarding."

"Thank you," he said, coming to his feet and collecting his personal items. After a short walk to the gate, he completed the check-in process, boarded the aircraft, and found his window seat in the first-class cabin. He was pleased to see nobody had been assigned the seat next to him. For the first time in days, he saw the finish line in sight. With escape almost assured, he felt as if he could take a relaxed breath.

"Good evening, Mr. Cunningham," the flight attendant said. "It's nice to have you onboard. May I offer you something to drink prior to take off?"

"Thank you. I'll have a tomato juice with no ice," he answered, while he settled into his seat.

Just as the flight attendant returned and placed his drink in front of him, a man in a dark-blue suit took the seat next to him. He was young with a baby face and a military crew cut. He didn't seem to have the profile of somebody who customarily flew first class. In no mood to talk to anybody, Cunningham turned away and checked his emails on his cell phone.

"Mr. Cunningham?"

"Yes."

"I'm Special Agent Mansfield with the FBI," he said, discreetly showing him his identification. "I'm sorry, sir, but I have to ask you to come with me."

Cunningham set his drink down. "I beg your pardon?"

"Right now, sir."

"I'm on my way to an extremely important business meeting. I'm sure whatever you want to talk to me about can wait until my return." He held his cell phone up for Mansfield to see. "I'd be happy to call Assistant Attorney General Davison. We went to law school together. I'm sure he'd be happy to clear up this misunderstanding. What was your name again?"

"Sir, you're welcome to make that phone call from our office as soon as we get there. But right now, I need you to step off the plane." Mansfield leaned in a little closer and, in just above a whisper, added, "I'm sure you'll agree the best way to handle this is with as little fanfare as possible. I assure you that you will be getting off this airplane with me. The way we accomplish that is entirely up to you, sir." Mansfield stood up and moved into the aisle.

As Cunningham joined him in the aisle, he inquired, "Do you mind me asking the reason you're disrupting my travel plans?"

"I think it would be better if we discussed that when we're outside in the terminal."

"And my checked luggage?"

"That's already been taken care of."

"For God's sake," he muttered. It was unlikely the other passengers in the area heard any of the conversation, but by the looks on their collective faces, it seemed obvious they were aware that something out of the ordinary was taking place.

Cunningham opened the overhead bin and brought down his carry-on luggage. He glanced down the aisle toward the exit. Another man, also wearing a dark blazer and a tie, stood there looking toward him with his clasped hands joined in a fig-leaf makeup. Cunningham had no doubt he was a colleague of Special Agent Mansfield's.

With a smirk, he said in a calm voice, "I hope you and your associates are on solid ground dragging me off this flight. I'm connected with more top-flight lawyers and influential people than you have hairs on your head. I assure you that a lame sorry-gram isn't going to save any of your sorry asses."

"Yes, sir," Mansfield said, pointing toward the exit. "This way, sir."

Without anything that even remotely resembled an unpleasant scene, Mansfield followed attorney Miles Cunningham down the aisle and off the aircraft.

SEVENTY-THREE

THE NEXT DAY

Jacey was crossing the skybridge on her way to her office when Andrea approached from the opposite direction.

"If you don't lose that frown pretty soon," Andrea said, "you're going to need a plastic surgeon to remove it."

"I'm trying, Andrea."

"I don't understand. You should be ecstatic. In the first place, you kicked the Peer Oversight Committee's butt; in the second, you were right about everything you suspected; and finally, Marc Saunderson's awake and doing great." She threw her hands up in the air. "For goodness' sakes, give yourself a break. Instead of sulking, you should be doing a victory dance."

"For some reason, I just don't feel like it."

"Maybe you just need a little more time, Andrea said. "By the way, whatever happened with Liam?"

"What do you mean? He finished his rotation on ped cardiology and moved onto his next one."

"I wasn't asking about his medical-school schedule."

"No, I didn't think you were."

"So?"

"I'm sorry to disappoint you, Andrea, but there's nothing juicy to report. He went his way and I'm going mine."

Leisurely nodding her head, she said, "Something tells me the final chapter's not written on this one as yet."

"You're a die-hard romantic."

"And proud of it. I gotta run. Let's have lunch later," Andrea said, dashing away.

When Jacey turned down the final corridor that led to her office, she saw a group of FBI agents clad in blue windbreakers, scurrying around. Most of them were holding either a cardboard box or a laptop computer.

Special Agents Grady and Kurdock emerged from the group. They spotted Jacey and strolled over to join her.

"How are you, Dr. Flanigan?" Grady asked.

"I'm fine. How's the investigation going?"

"I think we're off to a good start. A criminal conspiracy of this complexity involves a lot of people of interest and takes time. But hopefully by the end of the month we should see some indictments come down from the grand jury. They're mostly low-hanging fruit. But it's the best way to work our way to the top." His phone rang and he stepped away to answer it.

"What about Dr. Delacour?" Jacey asked Maggie.

"I think she's beginning to feel the walls closing in on her. We figure she'll be scrambling to make a deal in the very near future."

"What about the parents of these kids?" Jacey asked. "Do you think they'll be facing criminal charges?"

"That's hard to say. We've started interviewing some of them. The adoption process is painfully slow, and the expense can be astronomical. The attorney involved promised them a legally adopted baby at absolutely no cost to them. All they had to do in return was agree to allow the child to undergo an operation. Ultimately, it will be up to the Attorney General to decide whether she wants to prosecute any of them. Hopefully, she'll realize these are decent people who believed they were saving an infant from a lifetime of poverty and illness."

"And Tim Gatewood?"

"We doubt he was the victim of a mugging. We think the man who killed him was the same one who attacked you."

"Unbelievable," Jacey said.

"I'll tell you one thing; this is a case that I'm likely never to forget." Maggie craned her neck to look past Jacey. "You'll have to excuse me. I see my partner summoning me." She extended her hand. "Take good care of yourself, Dr. Flanagan."

"You too."

Jacey continued down the hall and opened the door to her office. In spite of having more than adequate reason to believe a number of physicians and administrators at MCHH had acted in a deplorable fashion, she couldn't help but wonder where it would all end. The accused would surely assemble an elite legal team—no doubt, the best money could buy.

She sat down at her desk and leaned back in her leather manager's chair. Her mind shifted to the endless legal gymnastics she knew would inevitably take place in the months to come. She wondered if the guilty parties would ever spend any real time behind bars when judgment day finally came. She sighed inwardly, thinking if all they got was a slap on the wrist, it would be an unforgiveable and tragic insult to the parents and children they callously harmed.

SEVENTY-FOUR

ONE WEEK LATER

Jacey made no secret of the fact that she was still seriously thinking of leaving MCHH and returning to Montana. A day didn't go
by that she wasn't beseeched by any number of her colleagues
to reconsider and join them in rebuilding the hospital's reputation, and more importantly, its excellence in children's cardiac
care. She had listened politely but remained intentionally eva-
sive about her plans.

With her cellphone pressed to her ear, Jacey exited the hospital and walked out to the curb to wait for her ride home.

"I'm still not sure," she told her father.

"Well, you're certainly in a unique position."

"What do you mean?"

"You have a rare opportunity. Just because MCHH was the victim of some unscrupulous people doesn't mean the institution's
core values aren't still there somewhere. Being part of resurrect-
ing the hospital to what it once was could be very fulfilling."

"That's what I love about you, Daddy. You could find a silver
lining in the middle of a giant squall line. I'd ask you what you'd
do in my place, but you'd just tell me that I'm a grown woman
and capable of making my own decisions."

"Luckily for you, this is one of those decisions where there is no bad choice. Anyway, I'm not worried about you. I'm sure you'll figure things out."

"Thanks. I'll call you tomorrow."

Jacey put her phone back in her purse and was glancing down the street when she heard a familiar voice from behind her.

"Dr. Flanigan."

She turned around. "Yes, Dr. Gault."

"Please call me Adam."

"Thank you, and congratulations on being named as the new Chief of Surgery for the hospital. That's quite an honor. I'm sure you'll do a great job."

"I wish I shared your certainty. I'm glad I ran into you. Since being named to my new position, I've kind of been mulling something over that I'd like to speak with you about. Do you have a minute now?"

"Of course."

"I was thinking that our level of care would be improved if we named one of our cardiologists as the Director of the Pre-Surgical Care Unit. It would be a challenging position with a great deal of responsibility, so it would call for an excellent clinician with the promise of outstanding leadership skills. What do you think?"

"I think it's a great idea. We had a similar position at Montana Children's."

"I'm glad to hear you say that, because I was thinking of asking you if you'd be interested in accepting the position."

Open-mouthed, Jacey responded. "I'm . . . I'm extremely flattered, but there are other cardiologists on staff with far more experience and—"

"The position entails a lot more than just being an excellent cardiologist," he responded. "I've given quite a bit of thought to this, and for several reasons, I feel you're the best person for the job."

Jacey studied the uneasy look on Gault's face. Realizing that mending fences and basic human relations weren't his strong suits, she wasn't surprised he was uncomfortable. She did appreciate that since the moment he'd adjourned the Peer Review Committee, he'd been making an effort to improve things between them. She wasn't a person who held a grudge, especially when dealing with somebody like Gault who wasn't a naturally apologetic person. The position he'd offered her clearly intrigued her. It was the type of challenge she envisioned herself taking on as her career in pediatric cardiology progressed.

"I'm very honored by your offer. At the moment, my plans for the future are still up in the air, but in all honesty, your offer could affect my decision to stay on at MCHH."

"I was hoping you'd say that," he said, securing the top button of his coat. "Take some time to think about it. I won't name anybody until you've made a final decision. If you'd like to talk about it further, come see me in my office. Have a nice evening," he told her, as he started down the street.

When Jacey again thought about how hard that must have been for him, she caught herself smiling inwardly.

EPILOGUE

After a long day of seeing patients, Jacey exited the hospital, strolled to the curb, and looked down the street to see if her ride was approaching.

"How are you, Dr. Flanigan?" came a familiar voice from behind her.

When she turned around and saw it was Liam, and that he was wearing an FBI windbreaker with a large identification badge suspended around his neck, a modest grin spread across her face. Feeling mostly shocked, but a little amused at the same time, she took a couple of steps forward and reached for his ID badge.

"Special Agent Aiden Sutcliff. And here I thought you'd moved on to your next rotation. I had an inkling something was up."

"Really? That doesn't say much for my undercover skills. What gave me away?"

"Nothing specific . . . other than you having no instinct for medicine and being unquestionably the worst medical student ever assigned to me."

After a quick laugh, he pushed his hands into the front pockets of his jeans.

"My parents really wanted me to be a doctor, but I guess I wasn't cut out for it. So, after college, I went into the military. When I got out, I applied to the FBI." He raised a finger and added, "But in my defense, I did read a lot of pediatric cardiology, trying to keep up with you."

"Which naturally raises the question: Why were you at MCHH pretending to be a medical student?"

Scrubbing his chin for a few moments, he answered, "I've been working in the fraudulent adoptions section of the Bureau for the past five years. Several months ago, we got a tip about an attorney in West Virginia who was suspected of being involved in a number of illegal international adoptions. We discovered many of these children had cardiac problems and wound up at MCHH, so we decided to launch the hands-on phase of our investigation with an undercover operation here at MCHH."

"Did you have any idea what Dr. Delacour and the others were up to?"

"As much as we'd like to take credit for figuring that part of it out, the FBI knew nothing about a criminal conspiracy involving sham operations. That's one bow you get to take alone." Before Jacey could ask another question, he asked, "So tell me, Dr. Flanagan, what are your plans for the future?"

"They're kind of indefinite right now."

"No leanings at all?"

"Well, I'm considering moving back to Montana."

"I'm sorry to hear that."

"Nothing's definite yet. I have a lot to consider."

"From what I've learned about you, I'm sure you'll figure things out."

"Thanks. Do you mind if I ask you another question?"

"Go ahead."

"I assume there must have been several top-tier folks here at the hospital who knew who you really were and what you were actually up to."

"Actually, the only person who knew about my presence was Leslie Santoro. The FBI is usually pretty careful about those types of details," he answered. "I guess it was pretty fortunate for us that he wasn't involved in any of the criminal activity." He went silent for a few seconds, before clearing his throat and saying,

"I'm sure you have a lot more questions, so I'll make a deal with you."

After a cautious glance his way, Jacey said, "I'm listening."

"It would be a shame to spoil this chance meeting. So, why don't you let me take you to dinner? There's a great French bistro a couple of blocks from here. That way you can ask me all the questions you want, and we'll still have plenty of time left over to talk about things that, hopefully, aren't work related."

Jacey's eyes narrowed, and in spite of her best efforts to the contrary, the corners of her mouth curled into a smile.

"So, would you be my date, or an FBI agent on the job?"

"As of five minutes ago, I was off the clock."

"It would be a shame to waste such a strange twist of fate," Jacey said, sarcastically. "So, I guess I'll l take you up on your deal."

"Sound thinking."

"I have to give you credit for one thing. That's, hands down, the most elaborate plan a guy ever hatched to take me to dinner."

"It took me a while to come up with it," he confessed. Although there were dozens of questions playing in Jacey's mind that she was dying to ask him, she decided to hold off for the moment. There was no particular reason for her decision other than her intuition telling her it was the smart way to go.

"Are you ready?" he asked.

"I sure am."

"I should warn you . . . I'm not much of a first-date guy."

"Okay . . . but, if you're looking for a good first-date icebreaker, you might want to consider something else," Jacey told him with a chuckle as she took his hand and gave it a slight tug.

As they started toward the restaurant, Jacey couldn't help but wonder if by the end of the evening she might be one step closer to staying in New York.

ABOUT THE AUTHOR

Before Gary Birken first set pen to paper as a novelist, he was a full-time pediatric surgeon. Dr. Birken was born and raised in New York. After obtaining his medical degree, he studied general and pediatric surgery at the Ohio State University. Upon completion of his training, he moved to Hollywood, Florida, where he has spent his entire professional career at the Joe DiMaggio Children's Hospital.

When he's not in the operating room or story writing, Dr. Birken spends time with his ten grandchildren, pursuing his passion for aviation, and traveling. He is also an avid tennis player and holds a black belt in martial arts.

Made in the USA
Monee, IL
01 July 2024

61044848R00152